LAFAYETTE

This book is a work of fiction. Any names or likeness of individuals and localities are used loosely and are non-representational.

"For we wrestle not against flesh and blood; but against principalities, against powers, against the rulers of the darkness of this world, against spiritual wickedness in high places."

Ephesians, 6:12, Holy Bible, King James Version

LAFAYETTE

PROLOGUE

First and foremost, let me begin by saying that there is a supreme being—a God. It is a disputed issue among many, especially when the assessment of such a being's behavior and characteristics are considered. We have a tendency to debate the nature and purpose of God, such a being's gender, and most of all who God ultimately favors. However, my personal belief is not held as the result of a philosophical or theological debate, but rather as a progressive culmination of life experiences wherein my belief; my faith, has predicated miraculous happenstances of divine intervention.

Am I sinner? No, the foundation of my faith can be found in the Holy Bible. Am I saint? No, I would not consider myself to be one because I have experienced taking another person's life on numerous occasions—albeit for the sake of "justice". Daily I struggle with things that a lot of people may not struggle with. At the age of 30 I am still learning how to apply my faith when it comes to life and death. I don't always get it right, but as my wife often tells me I'm "closer to heaven today than yesterday".

Today was no different. My wife Faith and I started the day as we have every day for the past four years since we've been married—prayer. Afterwards we showered, ate breakfast and carpooled to work. It was both convenient and providence that we both became police detectives. Of course being five years older than me allowed Faith the opportunity to be on the police force longer than myself. Provision had been made that we were able to be partners.

Yet today was one of those days I wished that we were not detectives—or at least that she was not. Our department had been chasing a particular gang of bank robbers over the past two weeks, and with their heist today, our squad had caught a break in locating them. Outside the bank that these individuals had robbed other members of our squad managed to apprehend all but three who subsequently ran down the street to an old and abandoned parking structure. My wife and I followed pursuit, breaking away from our squad and the barricade we used to isolate the bank.

As we ran, our shoes clicked on the pavement mimicking the sound of our side-arms as we loaded them with ammunition clips. We briefly glanced at each other as a sign of understanding and commitment. It's not often that we brandish our weapons, let alone physically chase after criminals, but we made sure to watch each other's back. I was totally focused because Faith is more to me than just a partner; she's my rib, my confidant, my helpmeet. Her safety has always been my number one priority. So as we hurried up the levels, taking the drive way, I made sure to stay a couple of steps ahead of her in case something came our way.

We hear a car engine crank up and tires screeching thereafter. Seconds later a small SUV comes barreling down from an upper level aiming to run us over. Faith and I split instantly, dodging to the left and right respectively. She rolls too far and falls between a couple of guard rails down toward a lower level. I can tell she fell onto a car because I hear glass shatter and a car alarm go off.

By this time I'm back on my feet, firing my sidearm at the vehicle. I managed to hit both of the tires on the driver side of the vehicle causing it to crash into the guard rail. Once it crashed, the three bank robbers jumped out of the SUV and took off running down the drive way to the level below. That action makes me nervous because I know my wife is down there wounded and the bank robbers could very well take advantage of her and injure her further. Thus my pursuit engages again. But I miss something important—one of the bank robbers ducked behind their disabled vehicle once they jumped out of it to go on the run. I had barely a second to react before I was swung upon as I ran around the vehicle.

While exchanging punches with my attacker, blaring police sirens neared our location. It doesn't take me long to dispatch my attacker; a couple of upper-handed aikido-style punches and my attacker is leaning back against the SUV unconscious. I quickly hand-cuff him to the door handle and take off running toward the level below. Mid-stride, I hear an exchange of gunfire and Faith screaming out in pain. Coming around the corner I cry out to grab the attention of the last two bank robbers. I scold myself mentally because I was totally unprofessional about it. My reward was a bullet in my right thigh and left shoulder.

I fell to the ground and rolled under the nearest vehicle which the bank robbers lit up with bullets from their guns. I continue to roll under several vehicles until I reached one where I took up cover behind. A pause in gunfire occurs where the bank robbers attempt to reload their guns. During the pause, I hear one distinctive gunshot followed by someone falling to the ground. Apparently, my wife managed to shoot one of the bank robbers from whatever position and state she was in. Subsequently, the last bank robber started shooting again, but not in my direction.

The pain I was in from the gunshot wounds I carried was so severe I could feel myself starting to blank out, but I could not let that happen. My wife was injured, probably more so than me, and she was still in danger. I had to get up; I had to make it over to save her. I couldn't lose any more loved ones in this life. I prayed and mustered enough strength to get up and run around to the gunman, and before he realized it I was tackling him down to the ground.

He punched me, I punched him. We rolled and I thrust my knee into his side, we rolled over and he did the same to my side with his knee. The moment he got the upper hand in our fight, I saw him pull out a switch blade from his pocket. He thrust the knife toward me but froze in mid swing. It didn't occur to me until a moment later that he froze in response to a gunshot. I pushed him away and he fell over motionless. With much effort I rolled over to look back up the parking garage floor to where I heard the gunshot come from, and all I saw was Faith laying on the ground—her eyes closed, her hand firmly gripping her sidearm. It wasn't but maybe a few seconds after that wherein my vision all faded to black and I began to dream.

LAFAYETTE

Desiring to have somewhat of a formal meeting with my Maker, I waited until the pastor and clergy led the congregation in filing out of the building before I approached the altar. I needed to hear a personal word from the Lord. I needed God to speak to my heart. It's been a year since that fateful day with the bank robbers at the parking garage, and every day since then my wife and I have been trying to recuperate. While I thought my wife would be one to struggle with the mental aspect of recovery rather than the physical, in all actuality, I have been the one to struggle mentally—or should I say spiritually.

Though it was a mutual decision between Faith and the police department for her to resign following the incident at the parking structure, she still seemed positive. She only suffered with physical rehabilitation. Her spirit has been as vibrant and positive as ever throughout the whole ordeal. While I was deemed fit for duty about a month after the incident, my return to the department was strenuous mentally and spiritually. Up to that time, I was on a kind of career high. Everything was going great professionally; I was set to become the lead detective of my unit upon reaching ten years of service with the department.

My wife and I were doing great at home; though we didn't have any children yet, our bond could not have been stronger. We were both a couple of weeks away from vacation, but when that incident occurred we were set back a bit on all fronts. The recovery afterwards had been tough, and to this day I must admit—my life has not been the same.

My faith was all but shaken. It took me almost twenty years to cope with the loss of my father from a similar incident, so to experience the same for myself threw me for a complete loop. Now don't get me wrong, I still have hope and faith that I'm making a difference but I fear that even though I'm doing my best in this world to help save it, it is still not enough. People are still turning to drugs for their relief, running around trying to do things that can destroy their families; most not realizing that there is so much vanity in it all. However, I do know that the Lord does not blame me for the way His creations turn out and he does not ask me to win every battle for His greater good. I simply rest on the fact that God has blessed me to be what I am today, a living testimony.

Yet to calm my inner soul, to comfort my spirit, I always come to expressly give a small prayer of repentance and thanks. Unnecessary, probably, but I feel a stronger connection to the divine when I practice such formalities.

I ease down onto my knees before the altar; ignoring the dress of my dark blue suit, and while holding aloft a pair of sunglasses in my hands. No one could hear my prayer but God and I; which gave me reassurance in my sincere connection with Him. It didn't take but a few minutes to get across what I wanted to say and I end my prayer with a thank you and rise to my feet to leave; bowing respectfully at the indescribable aura I feel hovering above the raised pulpit area.

As acute as my senses are, for some reason I don't notice Pastor Anderson's presence until I turn around to leave. We meet halfway down the center aisle of the modest sized church.

"Welcome home, son," he says fatherly. A tone of voice I haven't heard from the mouth of a man in a long time. The shorter, middle-aged man shook my hand firmly upon my offering.

"Pastor," I reply in my usual somber tone of voice laced with a mild Cajun accent.

"You returning to your job as well?" he asks me.

A year ago I would have hesitated; even now I'm slow to speak. "I must, sir, if this city is to be saved."

"Can one man save this city?" Pastor Anderson prods.

"If God is helping him—yes," I say.

"Is God helping you, son?" Pastor Anderson looks at me with a smiling gleam in his eyes.

"I wouldn't be alive today if that were not the case." Turning back toward the altar, I stare wondrously upon the embroidered cross in back of the pulpit and hear a small voice whisper in my ear. Honestly, I could not understand it at the moment but I knew it was meant to reassure me later on.

"Then you just might be the man by whose hands God will save this city."

I receive a further word of encouragement from the pastor before eventually making my way outside. Standing at the top of the stone steps just outside the entrance of the church, I notice several members yet chatting around in the parking lot. Considering the simplicity of their lives, I smile to myself, and count them as extremely blessed with ignorance. Slipping on my sunglasses, I head for my wife's car at the end of the parking lot.

A great woman my wife is. Faith and I have been married for almost five years—but have seen each other through the best and worst of times. For the past year since the parking garage incident, I have been residing in Dallas, Texas on assignment with a multi-state drug enforcement task force, and during that time Faith had made it a point to visit me often—she even stayed with me for four months, just to look after me.

I also think of my dog, Peter, as I hit the freeway, heading to my home—one of the many apartments of a contemporary-living complex in west Little Rock. Peter, an older Labrador retriever, has the most remarkable intelligence a dog could ever have; which I think has something to do with him being around Faith and I.

My wife and my dog, two blessings of God I am thankful for every day of my life.

The large and spectacular green mountains circling Chenal Valley are picturesque as they sit under the blue skies this afternoon, brightened by the beaming orange disk filling the horizon west of the small valley. I had to flip the over-head visor down and to the left for risk of being blinded by the late august sun. Nevertheless, I admire the spectacle of it all because I know the next three weeks will bring cooler temperatures for the state and that her pine trees' leaves will begin turning brown and falling off—a seasonal difference becoming of a seasonal change.

I pull into the first parking space I see nearest to the entrance. Turning the car off, I call up my brother—an assistant district prosecutor—on my cellular phone. I get his home phone's answering machine so I leave a message. "Duke, this is Sam. I'm back in town now, so I'll see you later, brother." I hang up, deciding against calling my alternate squad partner, Toni Vaughn.

Five years Toni and I have worked together and she still hasn't come to completely trust me or utilize the personal advice I've given her concerning her troubled life.

Enough, I hear my heart say. I climb out of the car with my duffel bag and head down the sidewalk to the entrance's glass double doors.

I knew my heart was right to have me shut off thoughts about the world. I have a tendency to bring work home, forgetting that once I take the badge off there's nothing else I can for the day. I have worked myself nearly to death on several occasions worrying about things I can never really change, even though it seems to be God's plan for me to constantly deal with it. I guess I still have yet to learn anything from it really because patience is a virtue that I have yet to fully master.

However, God has always managed to blanket me with love, joy, acceptance, and comfort through my wife Faith—who was waiting for me as soon as I stepped in the door of our third floor, studio apartment.

"Sam!" Faith cries hurrying across the living area, her arms spread out wide.

I toss my bag aside and close and lock the door behind me. Faith jumps into my arms and I hoist her up, ignoring the pain I feel up my spine, but extremely happy about seeing her again. Faith shares the same ecstatic emotions. She wraps her arms around my neck and her legs around my waist in a lasting embrace. She takes my sunglasses off and tosses them aside to ardently kiss me while staring into my eyes. It's not long before she feels the welt on the back of my neck and I explain to her it was a gift from a criminal I had chased to New York. Her eyes adopt that certain gleam that always seems to convey her innermost feelings.

"Sam, I'm glad you're home," she says. I knew she meant it because I could feel every inch of her body tingling with joy. The close embrace we held contained a spark that I had almost forgotten about.

"How are you feeling today, any pains or numbness?" I inquire, returning Faith's endearing gaze. Faith feared for my safety yes, being the lawman that I am, but my number one concern has been her welfare because of the injuries she's endured.

"I feel absolutely fine today, baby, and I'll show you why later on." Faith runs her hand through my brown hair still gazing at me with her sparkling, almond-shaped hazel eyes. "But, Monsieur Lafayette, don't you ever leave me again."

Her tender smiling expression melts my heart and I feel as if I'm falling in love with her all over again. "I wouldn't dream of it, mademoiselle," I tell her before kissing her again.

I cannot explain how but at six o'clock in the morning I woke up, glancing over at my wife's sleeping form before getting up to leave. Barefoot, I make my way out to my black baby grand piano in the corner of the living area. My fingers have long ached to tickle the ivories so I sit down on the bench seat in my pajama pants. It's not long before I start to play either, my fingers remembering their flow in making flawless strides over the ivories like the way an old knight of England remembers the strength in his fingers every time he grips his sword. First I start off with tremors of classical notes then add soulful ones in to my liking.

My mother taught both my brother Duke and I how to play the piano and she did so with such reverence for the both of us, always urging us to perform if only for our self-esteem; especially after our father was murdered. But what a blow it was to my self-esteem when she was kidnapped on the very day I had a recital in college. Without a doubt though, Duke and I have been searching for her relentlessly ever since.

I hope to find her someday. It is one of the few reasons why I still play, to remind myself of why I'm still a detective. I cannot say the same for my brother. Even though he is less taciturn than I am, he doesn't readily show his emotions, and he accepts whatever comes his way without conditions.

I play for an hour and a half, heightening the tempo at regular intervals until Faith presses herself against my back and runs her hands down my chest to make her presence known. Of course I'm sure she's faintly aware of the fact I heard her padding across the floor.

"Bringing back sad memories, Sam?" she says in my ear.

"You know me, sweetheart. I seem to revel in memories," I quietly tell her.

Faith leans closer onto me and whispers in my ear, saying, "Christians do not live without some form of hope."

I smile. "—Or 'faith'."

"Baby, you need to quit." Faith seemed reluctant to let go of me but she does so anyway wearing one of my shirts and switching her hips while heading toward the bathroom.

I chuckle in amusement and head after her—but the phone rings. I head instead over to the kitchen counter and pick up the phone just as Faith turns on the shower.

"Lafayette," I manage to say.

"Hey, Sam, it's me Toni. I'm glad to know you're back in town," my partner, Toni Vaughn says. "Look, I'm sorry to put a damper on your return but your presence is needed on a major case."

I sigh heavily before replying, "Toni, can't the captain handle it?"

"*We* need your help, old friend," she says adamantly.

I jump slightly when Faith wraps her arms around my waist and lightly kisses my shoulder. She is covertly telling me to hang up the phone and join her in the shower, however, I relay to her what Toni is saying and it sets her on unease.

"Um, Toni, I'm on my way." I hang up the phone and turn to look at my wife's expression. It was impassive but her watery eyes belied her inner conflux of emotions. I pronounce her name softly and try to hold her but she brushes me off.

"You don't have to console me, Sam. I understand you have a job to do," Faith says.

I pull her close despite her protests. "I will be back for you, sweetheart."

Faith raises her head, bringing her face within inches of mine. The gleam in her eyes is noticeable and heartbreaking. "Make sure that you do."

I reply, "Okay, I know it isn't much, with me being just a man and all, but you have my word."

LAFAYETTE

Toni wasn't lying when she had said a major case was being inestigated. After arriving at the mayor's estate by patrol car I find that my entire police squad is on the scene canvassing the premises under the direction of the crime scene unit. I eventually make my way up the paved drive to the secluded and doubly gated home of Mayor John Rosenfelt who, as I've been told, was murdered last night.

I notice Toni talking with the chief crime tech and I catch her attention while standing off to the side. Toni's wearing jeans and a leather jacket over a small tee; which I'm sure she thinks is cute.

"Hey, Sam," she starts as she approaches me. "This is bad. Late last night someone apparently broke into the mayor's house and murdered both him and his wife."

I mask my wince of sympathy and take off my sunglasses to appear surprised.

"Toni, where is Ryan?" I ask.

"He's in the house—mayor's study, Sam, talking to the Captain," Toni says quietly. "He's the real reason why I called you though."

I nod and say, "I know, Toni." I head inside slowly then. Through the living room and large kitchen I walk cautiously, eventually making my way into the late mayor's study sitting just off the patio area. I note several lab techs going over the patio grounds but do not disturb them; my attention focused completely on my friend Lieutenant Mack Ryan—whose stepbrother was the mayor.

The middle-aged, graying haired man turns away from the mahogany desk to give me a certain look. I know the look very well because he's given it to me every day of the five years—and counting—I've worked with him. The look is one of sadness and expectation.

However, I have not the answer to his unspoken question.

"Gentlemen, we have a serious problem here," says Captain Jacob Brooks, an older, balding gentleman of African descent, walking in from another room.

Captain Brooks' presence is a very magnetic one. Whenever he walks in a room everyone is instantly drawn to his demeanor. One thing I've always noticed about him is his father-like character he carries in his conversations—something I've become to associate with his extensive experience of both personal and professional natures.

"How so?" I ask.

"I just got a call from the assistant chief of detectives—he's going to be shadowing the squad all this week," Jacob explains resignedly. "He says it's just to see how our operations run, but I know it's just because of this case."

I mask a slight chuckle. Personally I am not surprised that the administration wants to put a tighter leash on our squad. For the past five years, with every high profile case we have worked, the administration has deemed it necessary to assign someone to monitor us. Overall, the department has never liked our particular squad—which was started by Jacob and the chief of police six years ago at the behest of the then mayor. In a political move, the assistant chief of detectives made it a point to distance himself from Jacob and the squad. It was rumored that once the mayor's term expired our assistant chief of detectives would disband our squad and send everyone back to their respective origins within the department and retire Captain Brooks. However—we solved all our cases and contributed significantly to the sixty-percent reduction of crime.

"Here we go again," I say somberly.

"Yep," Mack adds. "Here we go again."

I look toward Captain Brooks again with curiosity. "Why are we here sir?"

"Because, Detective, preliminary evidence suggests the murders were committed by a suspect your squad once arrested. Dallas Carter." The presence of the county Sheriff Mike Fletcher is unmistakable as he voices his arrival, wearing an obviously expensive black, double-breasted suit; with him is my partner, Toni and my brother, Duke.

"Welcome back, Lafayette." Fletcher offers me his hand to shake, which I ignore, side-stepping over toward Duke whom I give a curt nod of acknowledgement.

Fletcher chuckles at the intentional discourtesy. "Well, he hasn't lost his southern charm." He turns toward Captain Brooks, adopting his friendly routine. "Well, Jacob. I'm sure you are aware of the conflicts of interest with this case?"

"You mean because of my second-in-command," Brooks says sternly.

"Yeah, that." I perceive Fletcher to have a second—and devious—agenda for showing up here. "I could remind you of protocol, but you already understand that what we have here is a very political case and it would behoove you to hand over the reins to me—if only for the sake of peer pressure."

I make a move to step in the conversation but my brother Duke beats me to it. "It would behoove *you*, sheriff, not to overstep your boundaries here," he says with as much conviction and passion as I've ever seen him possess.

"We're all on the same side, counselor," Fletcher retorts.

"And?" Ryan asks pointedly.

"I'll contact your squad later." Fletcher turns to leave but only gets to two steps before he's blocked by my presence. I do not move for him immediately, but when I do he gives me a warning-like glare.

A moment later Toni, Duke and I meet up out beside Toni's unmarked car. I notice that it is extremely sunny out and slip my sunglasses back on.

"Who got here first, Toni?" Duke asks.

"A deputy sheriff followed by me and the captain about five minutes later since we both live around the corner," Toni answers. "But guys, are we sure that what we think is happening is really happening?"

Duke and I meet each other's regretful look of acceptance of the facts. I, however, am now compelled to do something about it. I ask both Toni and Duke about everything they know on the case at hand. Toni tells me that not only did the crime scene unit respond to the sheriff's call but that they are filing their investigation under the sheriff's purview—which I do not find surprising, but disturbing.

"And, Sam, you remember Dallas Carter?" Duke inquires.

"How can I forget him?" In fact that is impossible. Five years ago, one of our first cases led us to one Dallas Carter who fought with conviction as a police officer to arrest a man who allegedly murdered his wife, kids, and partner. But when the suspect was acquitted on all charges Carter became so ill-tempered that he snapped and eventually went on a covert killing spree of everyone involved in the case. Eventually, I caught him after a few slip-ups on his part and despite his advances to kill me. I handed the case over to my brother to prosecute, however, and Carter was sentenced to life without the possibility of parole. However, the question now becomes how could Carter have done this?

Duke recalls the case as vividly as I do but he adds an element to our current case that I did not totally expect. "With the mayor dead and no one under him to take his place, the city council will assume temporary authority over the city government—and with Roger Camden as senior council member…well you know the story."

Looking away I give a sarcastic smile at hearing the egotistical councilman's name. I have actually met the man once, during one long internal investigation of him and his office, an investigation that I was assigned to, and which unfortunately turned up nothing.

"And you know he'll issue an injunction to have you all removed from the case; which means you know who'll really be in charge of the case. And of course I won't be the prosecuting attorney assigned to it," Duke adds. "Evil dwells in high places these days."

Toni scoffs and folds her arms against her chest. "Every time we get together to save the day, things just start looking grim from the beginning," she says.

I say, "For one reason or another."

As one, the three of us glance at Fletcher as he walks proudly down the driveway and approaches the chief crime tech. He speaks quietly to the older woman of Caucasian ethnicity, until she nods twice at him, quickly and respectively.

"You guys don't have a lot of time to make any headway with this thing," Duke says.

I say again, "For one reason or another."

Toni and I immediately leave afterwards with the understanding that Duke will keep company with Ryan and the captain until further notice and with the knowledge that this particular case is going to be a really intense one.

Just as smoothly as I had slipped my sunglasses on at the late mayor's estate I take them off in the autopsy room of the one and only state crime lab. "Glad to see you, Doctor Davis," I tell the large balding man of fair complexion examining the Rosenfelts' bodies.

"The hero has returned," Davis says. "It does my heart good to see you again, Monsieur Lafayette."

I offer the older man a slight smile and a curt nod. "What do you have for me, sir?"

"Basically, everything that's in the preliminary and what I've already told the sheriff's people," Davis replies.

"You gave the sheriff the preliminaries?"

Davis' features took on an apologetic look. I'm sure he regrets his actions but what is done is done. I urge him to go on with what I needed to hear.

"The Rosenfelts were both shot in the chest but whereas the mayor was killed in-stantly; Mrs. Rosenfelt died from asphyxiation. I still haven't retrieved the bullets yet," Roberts explain.

To me the thought of someone going to such lengths to kill a woman is more than heartbreaking…it is troubling. Women should be the most valued creatures on earth, especially a good woman. A good woman will help you back up when you fall—and I can definitely attest to that in the case of my beloved wife Faith. Nevertheless, I continue to listen to the doctor, while making a mental note to drop by my wife's restaurant, Milan-Lafayette's, to tell her how much I love her.

"But get this—there looks as though there is a significant time lag between her being shot and expiring."

"Why? She didn't die fast enough?" I look over the late Mrs. Rosenfelt's body un-easily.

"She was strangled, Lafayette."

I cast Roberts a distasteful glance before heading toward the door. But when he gives me well wishes on catching the bad guy I give him a solemn nod of appreciation and head on out the door.

In the corridor I find my partner's short, lithe figure maneuvering through the bustling throngs of crime scene investigators toward me. I meet her half way and we duck into a corner to speak at a normal level.

"They're still running DNA," Toni says, frustrated.

"A monster did this," I add, gritting my teeth. Such an act as the one in question is indeed terrible but that's the way our wicked world is beginning to operate. I, however, just try to ignore the severity of it whenever I can while trying to prevent it the best that I can. I pause and look away off into the distance. Toni notices this telltale gesture of mine for what it really means.

"What are you thinking, Sam?"

"Dallas carter was sentenced to life, wasn't he? So who let him out to see daylight?" I reply.

"Well I think he was granted permission to attend his mother's funeral."

I nod. "Someone with a badge or office had to give that kind of clearance. Also that someone would have had to have some serious political power, Toni."

"And that someone would have to have had a reason to want the mayor and his wife dead." Toni catches on quick, which I have always admired.

"Would you be kind enough to drive us to the offices of the state parole board?" I ask her.

She smiles. "Of course."

I slip on my sunglasses. "Thank you."

In route to the multi-level corrections' office building near the downtown area of the city, I ask Toni about what has transpired during my absence. Her response makes me chuckle.

"Well, first off you're good at what you do but when you leave…well, everything goes to literally hell as we know it. I mean everyone is just more inclined to commit a crime when you are gone, Bobbie, Lil' John, the entire Roc Valley gang, and even the South-side Lords."

"How about the recreational center my family set up?" I ask.

"You'll have to drop by and see for yourself when you get a chance, Sam," She says in her usual southern drawl. "Oh and did I mention Jack and Rebecca are back from their undercover stint with the FBI? Yeah, they finally caught up with San Diesel after ten months of grunt work."

"No, ma'am, but I'm glad you finally mentioned it to me. Our friends deserve to get a little relief after what they've been through."

We exchange a mutual glance of admiration just before pulling into the parking lot of the state corrections' office. We get out and head inside. At the receptionist's desk we ask to see the man in charge, of course, but are redirected to a senior staff member.

"I'm Detective Vaughn, and this is Detective Lafayette. Do you know when any member of the board will be free to speak with?" Toni asks the elderly, white haired man, with a contemptuous look in his eyes.

The man addresses his answer only to her. "Don't know. Most of them are out of town and the others are in a meeting," he says.

I decide to speak up to get to the point, unintentionally upsetting the man. "Well, we don't really want to bother them. We just wanted to ask a few questions for the sake of a case we're working." It was as if the man did not want to hear me; he only paused, uttering something under his breath, trying to avoid making eye contact with me.

"Sir?" Toni prods politely, understanding as well as I, the man's problem.

I take my sunglasses off and step closer toward the shorter man, speaking in a low voice. "Sir, I have just as much right to walk around as you do, maybe even a little more if you consider the heart. However, your repulsive attitude toward people like me does not surprise me, nor will it change the fact that I am right here, right now. What we as police officers need from you and all we ask for is your complete cooperation."

I realize I could've been more threatening but for some reason I have never seen the extreme need for it…or police brutality. I pity many of my brothers in arms for even resorting to such tactics—because there is always a better way.

Besides, the man before us complies and even tells us his name, Ted Dotes. And as he leads us to a small office and file cabinet room, I make a mental note to pray for him: that God would take up residence in the man's heart.

"It landed on my desk anonymously for me to erase or file in confidential last week but I haven't gotten to it yet," he says picking up a file from his desktop and handing it to me instead of Toni. I tell him it's okay to give it to Toni, but he insists and I relent. He then heads out the door, saying, "Take your time…but don't get me into trouble."

"That's one up for ebony," Toni quips after Dotes leaves.

I offer her a small smile at her. "Yes, I guess it is, ivory."

Looking over Carter's file I find the most upsetting thing: someone had indeed lobbied the governor to grant him leave to attend his mother's funeral, which resulted in him escaping from custody. I tell Toni what I find. "Look here, Toni, that someone who talked to the governor is listed here as a wealthy old friend of Carter's."

"Willard Devlin," Toni notes the name. She looks up at me curiously. "Perhaps an avenue to search?"

"Perhaps." I glance at my watch to check the time and notice that I'm late for a meeting--or at least that's what I tell Toni.

She shakes her head at me incredulously. "Only been on the clock for six hours and you're already ditching the job."

"Six hours is still too long. Besides, I've already filed this in my photographic memory in case we need to look back over it," I state. We lay the file down on the desk and head back out the way we came. On our way out we wave at Dotes who seems to be more appreciative of his atmosphere.

At first I was calm and relaxed on our way out the door—Toni leading the way to our unmarked car—but for some reason this feeling comes over me, an alertness that assaults my senses. I soon find out why when a large gray box van came whipping around the corner and into the parking lot. The second I see the driver roll down his window and aim a gun in our direction I yell ahead to Toni while breaking into a run toward her. The bullets I hear popping the ground behind me drives me to move faster than I have ever done before, and not just for my sake but for Toni's as well because she was unprotected and easily a target. Toni turns around just before I jump her across the hood of our car to take cover down beside it. The gunman riddled the car's driver side with bullets in a seemingly desperate attempt to get us. We waited until the shooter stopped before moving, which did not take long. Disregarding my partner's swearing while with-drawing my sidearm from my shoulder holster; it takes me very little effort to jump back over the car and chase after the van on foot, shooting at it; Toni falling in close behind me. I run as fast as I can again but this time it is to place the van's license plate number and to cause as much damage as I can for positive identification of the van later on.

The driver was driving madly into oncoming traffic, which slowed his getaway considerably. Notably I hit the driver through one of the rear windows and he steps on the gas, disappearing from view when he rounds a corner five blocks ahead.

"This case is bigger than I thought," Toni says. I'm at a standstill in the middle of lunch break traffic when she appears at my side. I'll take her to the hospital for the bullet graze in her shoulder momentarily but for now I wait long enough to catch my breath.

And as for this case…it's smaller than I thought.

LAFAYETTE

"No, Faith, I'm Okay. Toni's just fine. I will be home shortly," I tell my wife via my cell phone. Somehow or another she had got wind of what happened to Toni and I. I could tell from the tone of her voice that she was concerned for us—me in particular. I try to tell her everything's all right but even after years of being married to me, instead of developing a tolerance for what I go through on the job, Faith has grown more frightful of it.

"Sam, I want you home as soon as possible," she says adamantly.

"Faith, I will be home when I can, you know that—"

"I know, Sam. But I miss you and I want to hold you close so I'll know you're safe."

"Faith, 'you are mine and my desire is toward you', I will be home shortly," I tell her softly.

"'Make haste, my beloved, and be thou like to a roe or to a young hart upon the mountains of spices'." Faith hung up after that, leaving me with an awkward silence.

"Why the long face, partner?" Toni asks, a nurse holding her hand and helping her out onto the curb. I turn away from the curb just outside the hospital to see her, noticing her arm in a sleeve.

"Um, Toni, I'm going home and I think you should do the same," I tell her with as little expression as I can to belie my intentions.

"C'mon, Sam, it's only two o'clock in the afternoon. And you know we have very little time on this before it gets ugly."

"That's why we need to take an early break before it gets ugly," I reply. I really want to end this day now, on a good note. But considering the evils that are against me I may just end up breaking my promise to my wife—and that I cannot have.

The Taxi Cab I had called while Toni was in surgery finally pulled up to the curb behind me. I reached back and opened the door for her. "See you tomorrow, Toni."

"You're really through for today?" Toni asks, moving toward the cab. I nod and usher her into the cab as politely as possible. She smiles then as if she's figured me out. "You want to get home to Faith, don't you?"

I nod certainly, though it wasn't entirely the truth. I've learned over the years that substituting lying with omitting the truth occasionally helps my case of privacy. This, I am quite sure that Toni knows. It's why I have her riding off quickly in a Taxi Cab.

My brother Duke pulls up a second later to give me a ride to the building I used for after school youth projects I started after my college years. The ride is a slow and de-pressing one through the urban neighborhoods I've been trying to save. Streets are pot holed and littered with trash. At two in the afternoon, kids were already out, playing in the streets.

I have a feeling I'm not going to like what I see when we turn the corner onto a high traffic road ahead.

"Brace yourself, Samuel," Duke says. It is the only comfort, though a small one, I get. Around the corner is a large building that looks as if it was a thousand years old. The place I once knew to be a community center for youths after school was now a run down building with busted out windows, bullet riddled siding, and a large foreclosure sign on the front doors. Duke pulls the car up to the front-entrance where I can get a good look at the city-provided lock on the doors. I slowly get out of his car and approach the crumbling building, anger racking my nerves.

"I'm sorry, Samuel," Duke says solemnly standing behind me. "But I fought against hell and high water to at least keep it standing; you know who I was up against."

I know Duke tried to step in during my absence as best he could but this dying city is more corrupt than either of us had thought was even possible. What made it sadder was the fact that Duke and I were among the few who were trying to do something about it. I mean really, who would purposely shut down a place meant to aid the city's youth? I bang my fists on the doors to satisfy a deep-ridden anger.

"Come on, Samuel, let's get you home to Faith." Duke says, trying to console me by placing a hand on my shoulder. I comply with getting back in the car; promising myself that I was going to fix this shameful act—for the sake of the children.

As we drove I got a call on my cell from one of the junior officers in my squad. Answering her call, she told me the address registered to the license plate number I got from the vehicle someone tried to use in the drive-by on me and Toni earlier. The news perturbed me even more.

"Thanks for the ride, Duke," I tell my older brother after getting out at my apartment complex. I reached through the window and shook his hand.

"Alright, Samuel. Take it easy." Duke sits back up behind the steering wheel and slowly drives away. I can't help but to think about his personal state of mind right now. He must be feeling some sort of guilt about failing in his daily struggles within the legal system. Of course I sympathize with my beloved brother, but even though he is older than I, sometimes I find myself worrying about him as if I was the older brother.

Looking toward the sky I notice the sunny evening skies beginning to cloud over. A moment later I head inside with my head lowered. Upon entering my apartment, I find Faith washing dishes with a definite worried care, and soft spiritual melodies playing over a radio nearby. I close the door quietly and sneak up behind her. I wrap my arms around her waist, which makes her jump and turn around poised in one of the many defensive moves we learned back at the academy.

Seeing that it's me, she giggles and reaches over to the radio on the counter and turns the volume down. "Sam, you know I don't like it when you do that," Faith says trying to bring her breathing back to normal. She curls her long tousled hair back behind her ears using one of her index fingers. I, however, continue to look at her with an endeared, steady gaze.

"I'm really glad you're home though. Why don't you just—" Before she can get out another word I "jump" her. I pick her up while kissing her and take her over to another part of the kitchen counter. Sitting her down on the counter, she pulls away, giggling again.

"Saaam," she croons leaning back on the countertop. "I'm going to get you for attacking me like this."

"Now?" I reply softly, looking at her with a subtle expression. "Yes, now would be good."

Sitting forward, she brings her face within inches of mine. "Your mother warned me about you—that you were going to be trouble."

"Me? Touble? Noooooo," I reply.

Faith wrapped her arms around my neck. "You think you're funny." After that she took my hand and interlaced our fingers while caressing my chin with her free hand. "You're safe now, baby. You're with me. I won't ever let anything happen to you. Even if you were in trouble, I'll always find you."

She met my knowing gaze and smiled, small dimples dotting her cheeks.

God, I love this woman.

LAFAYETTE

At Milan-Lafayette's the next day, the door chime sounds when I enter the diner's entrance, slipping off my sunglasses. I spot Faith taking orders at the counter and proceed in her direction.

Smiling she notices me and points me toward her office in back of the restaurant. As I walk into the back I could hear Faith instructing her staff to take over what she was doing so that she could join me in her office.

I was standing behind the door when Faith finally tip toed into the room, unfastening her apron. By surprise I took her, closing the door, and pinning her back against the wall where her arms were positioned behind her.

She smelled so nice that right now I wished I wasn't on duty. Right now I wish I did not have to meet someone out in the diner. Right now I wish I wouldn't have to chase someone out of an apartment across the street. Right now I wish I could just stay home with my wife.

However, I am on duty; I am meeting with someone in a few minutes; I may very well have to chase down someone; the light switch is on the other side of the door, and Faith would more than likely much more enjoy being in my presence.

"The course of true love never does run smoothly," Faith says; her breathing labored because of how close she was to me. She knew how much I wanted to be with her every minute of the day we weren't together. She probably even knows how much God would *like* for me *to* want her, but her assessment of our daily dilemma was very accurate.

"Indeed, sweetheart. Ignorance is bliss," I reply letting her go for the moment.

Faith takes off her apron and heads over to her desk to put it down. "And might I ask, why aren't you wearing your Kevlar vest?"

I knew I had forgotten something back at the station this morning.

"I guess my head isn't in the job anymore. It's taking a while to get back in the habit of things."

"You are arguably the most decorated policeman in this city's history, Sam, and at the young age of thirty as well." Faith perched herself on the edge of her desk. "You are still the best because you are a God-fearing man. Don't let anybody—including yourself—ever tell you different. Remember when we were partners and no matter what we did our motives were always questioned?"

"Yes, ma'am, I do remember." I check my watch.

"And so what if everybody who knows you has it out for you."

"And therein lies the problem," I say under my breath. "Everybody who knows me has it out for me."

Faith stands up and moves closer toward me gesturing with her hands while she spoke. "Not everyone. But the question you should be asking is do you have it out for yourself? Doubts and trifles aside; do you still believe in yourself?"

"As much as one could imagine; yes."

"Then why do you search for something you already have?"

"The look still in my eyes?" I ask softly.

Faith nods solemnly. "More so now than ever before."

I pause, considering Faith's statement. Faith's daily words of wisdom were indeed thought provoking but for the first time in my life I am at a loss for words as a response.

Eventually I let the first thing on my mind go out through my lips. "I think it has something to do with my mother."

"Are you sure?" Faith reaches out and grasps my hands to hold in her own.

I stare off into the middle of nowhere to keep my composure as well as to gather my wandering thoughts. "I, um, I'm not sure." I meet Faith's gaze slowly. "I need help to find out. Will you-"

"I am your wife, Sam. You don't even have to ask for my help, I will always be there for you." Seeing Faith smile that reassuring smile she has given me countless times—and that always works—makes me feel the most appreciative of having her in my life.

I now think I'm closer to what it is that I'm looking for.

After sharing a prayer with Faith, and a kiss, I make my way back out into the main part of the diner.

I get to a table near a window seconds before an arrogantly collected; red-haired gentleman by the name of Roger Camden arrives, meeting me at the same table.

"Familiarity breeds contempt, Lafayette," he says sliding into the booth and laying his briefcase down on the seat beside him. "And whether you know it or not you have caused me trouble ever since the first day we met."

"Hmm, that's strange; because since we first met I have had nothing but good intentions towards you," is my reply.

I slightly turn my head to look out of the window at the towering apartment building across the street, hoping to catch a glimpse of my unsuspecting target.

"Seriously though, as much as I enjoy our occasional banter, I do happen to have somewhere to be. So if you—"

"Sir, has anyone ever contacted you about a parolee named Dallas Carter?" I ask cutting to the quick.

Camden hesitated, but smiled to cover it up. "Nope. Can't say that anyone has, Detective."

Even without the spirit giving me insight I can tell that the man is lying—through his teeth.

Camden stares at me as if he knows what I'm thinking, a smug look on his face. "Come on, Lafayette, would I lie to you—a fellow crusader for the city?"

"Quite possibly—if it suited your interests, sir," I say as coldly as I can. Glancing out of the window again I see a gray, beat-up Chevy box van pull into the parking lot across the street. A shaggy-looking Caucasian male with his ear bandaged gets out and heads inside the apartment building, carrying a fast food order.

"You know, Lafayette, it's a good thing the sheriff is leading this case. It's so high profile that the crime's perpetrator—whom I assume is still on the loose—could very well inflict harm on members of your squad," Camden begins to illustrate. "Think about it. There's a guy out there, whom your squad has put away before, who is also a certified murderous lunatic, and who also knows everyone in the SCS personally."

I lock gazes with Camden slowly, his blue eyes cold and threatening, his voice resonating with a dark tone.

"I mean really, how would you feel if someone broke into your home just to scare you or even vandalized this restaurant? Perhaps this someone would even attack your wife over there-"

My reply is quick and forewarning, "Get out."

Camden feigns surprise at what I said so I reiterate, "Get out, now."

He gets up from the booth with his briefcase to leave but turns back to get in the last word, running a hand through his wavy, reddish hair. "Remember, Lafayette, play with fire long enough and it will burn you. You want to get rid of the monster plaguing the city, when it is the monster that the city feeds off of. The only way to get rid of the monster is to substitute it with another monster."

I reply with, "Good day to you, sir," which sends the man on his way. Upon his departure I glance over at Faith who seemed right at home placing orders from behind the counter, her face alight with joy.

God have mercy on the poor soul who'd dare harm her.

When the time came for me to cross the street I did so with renewed fervor, my sidearm held at the ready, my heart set on things above, honorable and pure things occupying my mind to keep me steady.

Inside the apartment building, at the door of my suspect's apartment I paused long enough to knock. Now, this would be the time that I would call for backup, but it has been a long standing habit of mine to rarely call for back up.

One John Xavier called out from inside saying, "Who the heck is it?" Well, in more words of course.

I step to one side of the door and answered, "Little Rock police!"

A gunshot blast blew through the door at mid-level.

Praise the Lord. He missed.

By now I am quite sure John has recalled my voice. You see, at another time, and at another place we attended the police academy together, but whereas I graduated, he did not—and I am of the opinion that this is what adds fuel to his inherited fire of hatred toward me and every other Lafayette from the black waters of Louisiana's bayous.

"I knew you'd come after me sooner or later, Lafayette—if you survived the drive-by," John says. I hear him drop the shotgun and run off into another room. "I've been waiting a long time for the chance to put you down!"

"John, I need to talk with you!" I took a chance and hurried into the apartment, ducking behind a dingy sofa. When John came out of what looked like a bedroom wield-ing a hunting rifle I trained my gun on him over the back of the sofa.

The dangerous part of this scene was that he had a more capable weapon than me, and my next position of cover was a bathroom five feet away. I didn't want to shoot him but I knew it could very well lead to that. Every time I kill someone, every time I force some-one out of this world it perturbs my soul—because another life has been forfeited without a chance for the individual's soul to be saved.

"Lafayette, you should have stayed up in New York," John tells me. "Always making things difficult for guys like me has finally led you to this point: death by an 'old friend'."

"John, there is no such things as 'guys like you'; in spite of the rich and promising life you were offered you chose instead to live a simple, degrading, and hopeless life," I tell John. "But I tell you what; if you put the gun down we can figure out how to get your life back on track. I fear for your soul right now, John. Trust me now, just as you did when we were at the academy together."

I note two places where I could shoot John to neutralize him—his trigger finger's arm or higher, in the middle of his brow. I must choose wisely for my sake because he has his gun aimed right between *my* eyes and though I value his life—wayward as it may be—I intend to make it home tonight.

"There are things at work here bigger than either of us, Lafayette. You ruined my life—your life should have been mine. There's gonna be so much glory in killing you before my father does."

The only thing he got right is the part of 'there are things at work here bigger than either of us'.

"I don't know about you, John, but I am going home at the end today."

"Screw you, you son of a—"

My heart filled with sadness; I choose the headshot, and John falls back into the doorway of his bedroom. I holster my sidearm and come to stand over his lifeless body. Staring at the grim eternal fate etched on his face, I pry the shotgun from his grasp. "Lord, I pray that you would have mercy on this man's soul."

Later on, I find myself standing in the lobby of my squad's department, looking out through the entrance's glass doors at the sunny tuesday evening. However, hearing the soft footfalls of my partner's approach I turn around to face my partner as she approached, while taking off my sunglasses.

"Sam, the captain wants to see you before we roll over to the sheriff's office," Toni says with apprehension, adjusting the sleeve on her arm.

"Have faith, ma'am," I tell her.

In the captain's office I wait until Brooks offers me a seat before I sit down. His second in command, Lieutenant Ryan is standing near the window behind Brooks. Ryan's facial expression teetered between one of boiling contempt and sadness. I cannot blame him seeing as how he's conflicted between the policies against him being involved with the investigation and how he wants revenge on the murderer.

"Sam, I want you to listen carefully," Brooks begins. "Mike may attempt to assign you as a special deputy in his office's homicide division for the duration of this investigation. This of course is meant to throw off suspicions of mistrust between his office and ours. But I do not want you to go along with it."

The captain's words mirrored exactly how I feel about the communication line between us and the sheriff's office. It would be unfair to bend over backwards to appease our counterparts in the sheriff's office when they have done very little if anything concerning keeping the serial crime squad in the loop, however, at the same time the perception of both agencies working together on a high profile case would help calm down the internals fears and apprehensions between the departments.

"Captain, I thought we were going to outrace Fletcher's office to the evidence. What, might I ask has changed?" I inquire.

Ryan sighs and, turning around from the window stares at me expectantly. "One of my friends in the Sheriff's office mentioned to me that they overheard a conversation between Fletcher and Xavier. From what they say, Fletcher is supposed to spearhead this case and sweep it under the rug. My concern is that we cannot win this one, Sam. Xavier is reaching like never before. We think that my brother's murder is being used as a catalyst for the war Xavier wants here. If we were to have a chance, we have to be compliant but also clever."

I glance at Brooks who simply lowers his head. I can tell he's been stressed lately. When he's silent, he is usually brooding about past situations that he feels could have gone a different way with the slightest of change of actions, especially when the monster is involved.

The described monster is one Fredrick Xavier—the most dangerous, wealthiest, and corrupt businessman west of the great Mississippi. He has plagued every city a relative of mine has ever resided in—long before they even arrived. From New Orleans and Baton Rouge, Louisiana to Fort Worth, Texas and even San Diego, California said monster has made a living on sacrificing those around him and destroying those who oppose him in order to gain control over city and municipal governments. I would go on to venture that his control over these government bodies is why he hasn't been convicted and sent to prison. My personal mission of course has been to put an end to his terror.

I lean forward and speak softly after considering the possibility of listening devices in the room—which I am sure there are. "Gentlemen, I want to do this my own way. Because if I do not, I believe a lot of people will get hurt. And I do not want that, I do not *need* that."

Brooks nods and stands up behind his desk, glancing at Ryan. He turns around toward the only window in his office and stares out of it contemplatively. "So you don't need the help of your friends to handle it this time around?" he asks.

"I do, sir." I stand up and slip on my sunglasses expressively. "But it would be best if the monster did not know that—we must let him believe that it is only me that he's fighting."

Ryan doesn't respond immediately after that, he purposely allows a short silence to pass by. "You do realize we won't be able to help you fully?"

"I know, sir." I watch the captain turn back toward me appearing both collected and remorseful.

"Sam, I need you to be careful. The last time Xavier reached out like this I lost your father and I was put out of commission for a whole year," Brooks says evenly.

"If my fate is similar then I will take God with me, sir," Is my solemn response before quickly disappearing from Brook's office.

Walking out into the parking lot, I find my partner and two other familiar faces by an unmarked car. One is a Hispanic woman with an ample figure and dark brown hair; the other person is a slightly taller Caucasian male, clean-shaven with a lean muscular build. All three offer me a smile as I approach.

"Sam, you remember Detective Sergeants Rebecca Sanz and Jack Dawson," Toni says. "Bec, Jack, once again, the great Detective Samuel Lafayette."

I shake the other detectives' offered hands. "Glad to have you two back," I say before heading around to the car's driver side.

"Sam, where are we headed?" Toni asks.

"We're going to check with the lead officer on Carter's reprieve detail. Then *I* have a meeting with Fletcher," I reply. I notice Toni's hesitance, her eyes darting in the direction of Sanz and Dawson. I appear confused for only a second knowing what she was silently implying. "Um, would either of you two lovely people want to join us?"

"I have some expense reports I have to file, but I think Mister Dawson here would love to join you," Sanz volunteered, glancing at Dawson with a smile.

Dawson shrugged. "You're not right Rebecca." I watch Sanz bid Dawson goodbye. Then Toni, Dawson, and I get in the car and drive off.

With Dan Carmichael being a lead agent within the department of corrections for the state, he was provided an office. Our drive to Dan Carmichael's store front office is a short one, with Toni and Dawson joking and laughing all the way. I participate every once in a while even though my mind is elsewhere—specifically dwelling on whether or not I can accomplish what I've been sent out to do in this world.

Once at our destination, it is eerily quiet as we enter the building. Our footfalls echo throughout the empty space.

Toni claims to have been here before and she takes the lead as we make our way into a short corridor of small back offices. Dawson follows Toni without precaution, absently looking around like a child. I, however, am very wary right now.

I slip off my sunglasses and withdraw my sidearm from the holster.

"Sam," Toni calls from the doorway of a small office. I come and stand behind both her and Dawson in the doorway. "He was here."

We find, sitting upright in his office chair, Dan Carmichael; a large dark spot centered on his chest and expanding.

I turn and bolt out of the building. On the sidewalk I pause to glance around through the busy metropolitan, downtown area. The sidewalk, lined with locals and tourists, bustling, served as an excellent opportunity for a potential murderer to disappear. A 'sixth sense' directs my attention to the city trolley turning the corner.

There is a tall, dark-skinned man jumping onto the moving trolley as if it was an emergency.

I glance back at Toni and Dawson who had followed me out of the building. "Toni, stay and call crime scene! Dawson, you're with me!" I take off running in the trolley's direction with renewed fervor, Dawson following close behind me. Seconds later we are surrounding the front of the trolley; shouting at the driver to stop. He did but our suspect jumped off and ran toward the riverfront pavilion just north of the locale outdoor trade and produce market.

In my hurry to catch up to him I run into a class of students on a field trip. The youths block me from my suspect resulting in him increasing his getaway field.

Out the corner of my eye I see Dawson—weapon drawn—running around the dragging youths to continue pursuit of the suspect. I'm distraught over this—but not for long. The class finally moves enough for me to take off again.

I am really getting a workout today. I can tell my dark gray suit is being worn with my body perspiring; however, it is clearly the least of my worries as I chase after my suspect.

Dawson and the suspect disappear from view as I follow them into the city's riverside park.

This I do not like. "Dawson? Dawson?" I call out. I hear scuffling coming from behind several large playground equipment sets and I run over, fearing the worst. As I approach, I see Dallas Carter punching Dawson out on the ground and getting up to run.

I let Carter get twelve feet away before ordering him to stop and put his hands on his head; my weapon trained on him.

"Is that you, Lafayette?" Carter turns to face me as if to disarm me with friendliness. "Long time no see. I've been meaning to tell you, I'm sorry about shooting you when we last met. It was very bad times back then."

"Dallas, I do not want you to run or resist arrest. Do you understand?" I ask firmly. "It could get you killed."

"I won't, Lafayette," Carter says coldly. "I'm sure you have enough problems from today."

"Why would he do this, Sam?" Toni asks me as I close the rear door of our squad car. Inside is Carter, handcuffed. "Why would he come here to kill this guy?"

"Carmichael had something to tell us," I tell her. "And I think I know what."

Dawson finishes talking to one of the crime scene techs in front of Carmichael's office and then comes over to Toni and me sullenly.

He is adamant about the job yes, but I am worried about him because of his total disregard in wielding his sidearm in front of the class of students we had ran into earlier. I take his apparent sarcastic and assertive demeanor to be a very integrated—and also dangerous—part of his character. Something I find not the least bit admirable.

"Jack, are you okay?" Toni asks him.

He offers a lowly grin. "Come on now. I do this for a living," he says. He glances at me and notices my look of apprehension. "Is there a problem Lafayette?"

"I think there might be, Mister Dawson." I turn back to the car and get in. Toni keeps me though from closing the door.

"You don't need anyone to help you book him?" she asks, eyeing Carter in the back-seat.

"Toni, I'll be fine. I'll meet you back at the station later," is my reply. "I need to speak with Fletcher alone."

"If you say so." Toni stepped away gingerly and I close the car door, start the engine and drive off.

I start off on my way to the station to book Carter. However, I decided to drive there as slowly as possible, because my former fellow officer was talking non-stop—and I wanted to hear what he had to say.

"I really didn't think you were going to get me again, Lafayette."

I give him a moment's glance in the rear-view mirror. "How's that, Dallas?"

The older darker-skinned man just chuckled. "I trained you, remember? It was just pure luck you caught me the last time, my limited knowledge of forensics notwithstanding. I had thought that this time around I could still be less meticulous concerning my actions since I'm being backed by some very powerful people."

"Oh?" I feign surprise. "Did these *very powerful people* ever visit you while you were in prison?"

Carter hesitates. "You know what; one guy did visit me—two weeks before my release. An old white guy—looked like an Italian—with slicked back black hair and a certain mischievous grin, you know?"

"I've seen him. But did he tell you who to meet with after you escaped your security detail?"

"A Mike Fletcher," Carter mumbles.

I finally pull into the station's parking lot, having to ease the car through throngs of reporters to get to the front entrance.

As soon as I park and get out I find myself surrounded by reporters with pestering questions. "Detective! Detective!" each one says, trying to get my attention.

"Detective Lafayette, are the recent crime sprees a result of your return or your long departure?" asks another. "You know the total number of murders since January is seventy-five; two-hundred and twelve since you were last here."

"Detective Lafayette, the strength of the police department now rests on what you and others find concerning the mayor's death. How is that affecting the Serial Crime Squad's investigation?" prods another.

"Detective, there are reports of un-cooperation between the department and the sheriff's office; are they true?" inquires another.

With much effort I get Carter out of the car, through the pressing crowds of reporters, and into the building, without even saying a word.

In the lobby I run into Ryan and Sanz who appeared to be guarding the entrance from the nosey people with cameras outside. Ryan nods at me with an appreciative stare at the same time Sanz ends a very animated conversation on her cell phone.

I turn Carter over to Ryan who assures me he'll take care of him. Respectively I nod and head out the door, back into the reach of the public.

"The Sheriff will see you now, Detective," says the female deputy behind the desk in the lobby of the sheriff's office minutes later.

I turn, on my heel, away from the entrance doors while slipping off my sunglasses and head for Fletcher's office. "Thank you, miss."

I step into the office and up to his desk slowly, pretending to admire the scholarly décor of the room.

"Just who the heck do you think you are?" Fletcher asks sitting in his chair behind the desk. His tone of voice doesn't completely catch me off guard. I knew it was coming; I just would rather avoid it if at all possible—it's quite irritating.

"Sir?" I feigned surprise.

Fletcher slowly rises to his feet, an oddly enraged expression displayed on his face. "At what point did you become the lead investigator on *my* case, Mister Lafayette? You and your squad have been working nonstop to close *my* case without *my* supervision," he fumes.

Despite Fletcher's self-centering rants, I respond calm and reserved. "It was my hope, sir, that what I and my colleagues find would be added to your already resourceful stockpile of evidence."

"What part of 'you work for me' during the course of *my* investigation, don't you understand?" Fletcher pauses to rub his brow timidly. "What you seem to not realize is that you've solved *my* case in the short time it's been open. I got the full report of the crime lab's evidence results back and it ties John Xavier to the Rosenfelts' murder."

"And it conveniently clears Mister Carter of the crime in question," I say.

"Yes, if you want to put it that way. You killed the guy responsible for murdering the Rosenfelts and for trying to whack you off. However, Carter is still a bad guy, and a bad guy *we* will take care of. Case closed."

I turn away purposely. "Or swept neatly under the rug."

"And also, you detective, may want to talk to your brother. Rumor has it; the DA's office has motioned your superiors to disband your squad. " Fletcher sits back down in his chair as if he had just fixed a resistant and nagging problem.

I look over his desktop with a glance but I take a second look once I see a scrupulous document with the name Fredrick Xavier on it. Fletcher casually turns the paper over as if I did not see it.

The information I've just received is all but jarring, all of my earlier suspicions having been proven correct. Carter was acquired to commit the murders in a fashion that resembled his previous ones but did not completely tie to his criminal background. Leaving instead suspect number two: drive-by shooter (John Xavier) to take the blame—that I am now realizing I was led into shooting.

Three questions have now been raised from my view of things. One: how is Fletcher tied to Fredrick Xavier? Two: why would Xavier sacrifice his own son? And three: why exactly were the Rosenfelts and Carmichael murdered?

"Good day to you, sir," I tell Fletcher as I turn to leave slipping on my sunglasses.

"Oh, and next time you try to bigfoot your way around in one of *my* cases, Detective, I'll have you arrested for interfering in an investigation," Fletcher informs me.

Taking my leave I offer the man a reluctant smile.

He is going to fall so hard from his high place.

On my way home I call Toni and tell her to schedule a squad meeting for tomorrow morning at eight o'clock. I also tell her to keep Carter in holding until I say different, no matter what.

It has been a long day to say the least but I do not swear at the Lord about it. In fact, if I had to do it all over again I probably would; of course after God renewed my strength.

"Uncle Sam! Uncle Sam!" Ella and Duke Jr. cry as I step into my apartment.

I haven't seen my brother's children in almost two years, and to see them now warms my heart.

The two hug me around my legs and do not let go. "We're happy to see you again, Uncle," says the oldest, Ella.

"I can see that, 'little detectives'," I reply. Glancing at Faith—who was in the kitchen preparing dinner with Rachel, my brother's wife—I notice her giving me a knowing smile, and I return one in kind.

"The hero is finally home," Duke states sitting at the counter. "Now we can eat."

I head in his direction once I'm free again, the children gluing themselves back to the television set.

"What are you talking about, brother, and your day has just begun with all the briefs you have to prepare for court in the morning." I flock to Faith at the sink and kiss her on the cheek, which she happily receives. I then turn to Rachel. "How've you been, Rachel?"

"Good, Sam," Rachel replies cutting celery sticks over the countertop. "Just keeping your brother in line."

I chuckle. "I know."

"Do you also know your pretty little brown hair won't stay that way for long?" Duke quips.

Taking off my suit jacket I circle back around to him and place a hand on his shoulder. "Only you received the premature gray hair trait, Duke," I tell him calmly.

"Okay you two," Faith interrupts. "Sam, honey, you go on and get settled in; I'll be with you in a second. Duke, leave your brother alone and help Rachel set the table."

"Yes, ma'am," Duke and I reply together, receiving amused expressions from our wives.

In the bedroom I toss my suit on the back of a chair and step over to my dresser where I place my sidearm, badge, watch, and sunglasses on top. I give up hope trying to find my prescribed medication and just lay down on my back on the bed, closing my eyes and allowing my thoughts to wander.

My work as an investigator is becoming more and more dangerous—especially as of late. I've had to do some clever and confrontational things before, but nothing like what I have to do now. I have come face to face adversaries in high places; I've had to end someone's life; and a monster from my past is threatening his return.

This I do not like even though it seems to contribute to God's big picture. I find myself thinking this way because more and more obstacles are surfacing and fewer victories are being claimed. God, what is the endgame here? How long will this go on? Am I making any kind of difference?

Lord; listen to me…I sound like a man without any hope or…

Faith comes into the room and closes the door behind her. I can hear her humming softly as she climbs on top of me, looking up at me, resting her chin on my chest. I don't even have to open my eyes to see the hint of her trademark smile which always lifts my spirits.

"I heard what happened to you after you left the restaurant today, Sam," Faith says. "Are you okay?"

"I wasn't injured," I reply adding a low rumble of a growl.

"I wasn't talking physically, sweetheart."

"You already know the answer to that."

Faith steeples her fingers underneath her chin in a contemplative gesture. "I know."

"I can't wait to just *sleep*," I say dreamily. "I'm very, very tired."

"You *are* making a difference. You're letting the world know that there are still good men fighting the good fight of faith."

"I know there are others out there like me, but how many of us are leaving a lasting impression?" I shake my head.

"They have their own story, Sam. Let's just live out yours—which I believe is absolutely amazing."

I chuckle a little. "Flattery will get you nowhere."

"Well, I guess we better get back to our guests then." Faith smiled mischievously.

"Mm-hmm," I say.

Faith climbs off, still smiling, and heads toward the door while I sit up on the bed.

"Faith, sweetheart, would you hand me my pills please? My eyes have gone all blurry."

"Sure," Faith replies, picking up my medicine bottle from atop the dresser. She brought it to me saying, "Come and get some water in the kitchen to go with that."

"Yes, ma'am," I reply, watching her as she left.

At the dinner table, with a delicious-looking meal served by Faith and Rachel, we eyed all we could eat. Duke said grace and we began feasting with joy and good company.

"So, Sam, how've you been?" Rachel asks. "Chasing criminals all over the country and trying to rebuild cities is hard work I hear. Weren't you in the news up there in New York for a while?"

Sitting opposite me at the other end of the table Duke helped spoon-feed his son who was sitting on a phone book in his chair just like his sister. "Yeah, Samuel, I have heard some interesting stories about your adventures," he says. "Care to tell any good parts about them?"

I take a sip of water. "There wasn't much good in Louisiana you know, but I can tell you this, there was great courage in the people I worked with when I was down there. We built some real bridges, both physically and socially," I say with a somber voice. "And while I was in New York a couple of detectives up there helped me catch the fugitive I was after; afterwards everything just cooled down and I was finally able to rest."

"Did you see any of the sights while you were up there?" Faith asks passing Rachel a couple of napkins for Ella.

Smiling I reach over and cover Faith's hand with my own. "Yes, ma'am, I've seen many sights while I was up there, but none compare to the sight I'm seeing now."

Hearing that, Faith blushed and looked away. Duke scoffed, and Rachel hit him play-fully.

"You know it's been a while since you've said anything like that to me, Duke," Rachel told my brother.

Duke cast me an unappreciative glare. "Thanks, Samuel, now you've made me look bad in front of my wife."

Masking a grin I reply, "You didn't need any help in that department brother."

The children giggled at their father and I think, at me as well, over the chemistry we shared—which I might add took many years to cultivate.

"Anyway," I began, as everyone continued eating. "So how's Peter doing, brother?"

"Oh, I don't have him anymore," was Duke's reply. "You see, I gave him back to Faith when little Duke junior here got too obsessed with him."

I glance at Faith. "I was letting mom and dad keep him, honey, you know, until you get settled back in," she told me.

"Hopefully," I say, sighing.

This time Faith covered my hand with hers and her eyes met mine. "Don't worry, Sam."

After dinner with my brother and his family—which consisted mostly of laughter and sidesplitting bellyaches—Faith and I bid them farewell and let them out.

Faith ended up standing at the kitchen sink washing dishes. I approached her quietly from behind and slip my arms around her waist while stooping to kiss her neck.

She playfully pulls away from me saying, "Saaam."

I say not a word, steadily kissing her, causing her to blush uncontrollably.

"C'mon, Sam, I'm washing dishes here." She swats at me, leaving soap bubbles on the side of my head.

I, however, do not give up. "I…love…you," I whisper in her ear causing her to quiver sensibly. "God's been really good to me with you."

"Sam," she manages to get out, "do you know what you're doing to me?"

"I'm doing nothing to you; it is God who's put it in your heart to feel good when your husband touches you. I'm just an instrument, remember?"

For a prolonged moment Faith just stands there letting me pin her against the counter while kissing her. She then turns her head to kiss me back with one loving, and tender kiss of her own.

"Faith," I managed to say under breath.

"Yeah?" Faith replies, obviously knowing that she now has the upper hand.

"You're mine now young lady."

Faith runs off, giggling, and as the very capable detective that I am, I fall into pursuit, laughing myself.

Strangely later that night, after enjoying being in love with my wife I sit up in bed waking from a terrible nightmare—in which the city is set afire. I'm breathing heavily and my heart is racing as I recall the frightening images of destruction and mayhem.

Faith wakes up a second later; I guess her spirit troubled by my mine. "Sam, what's the matter, baby? You're sweating."

"I don't know," I tell her. "One second I see myself running towards you, the city, and God; and the next you're gone, the city is burning and so am I."

Faith takes off her pajama top and uses it to pat me dry. "You're thinking too much of what you have to do as God's servant to save the city." she replies.

She could be right of course. Many a time when I am at rest, dark and worrisome thoughts yet find their way into my mind as I wonder about the next day. Though God indeed guards and keeps me, the enemy is still creeping in somehow—using my own thoughts against me.

My precious wife Faith is one of the few who understand that I won't be able to stand in harm's way much longer unless it is by God's doing.

"Come here, baby," she says tossing away her top. I let her pull me close to lie down next to her. She strokes my cheek with a tender caress while singing softly in my ear to comfort me.

LAFAYETTE

"Coffee?" I pointedly hold a Styrofoam cup before my partner Toni.

She takes the cup from my hands gratefully saying, "Thank you, Sam. And it's from the little lady's café & diner too."

I chuckle circling back around to my desk. "Carter still in holding?"

"Yep." Toni gulps down the coffee as if there was no tomorrow. I knew my wife's coffee to be good but I don't remember it being that good.

"Where's Sanz and Dawson?" I ask, clearing my desk.

"Not in yet. And it's ten minutes before the meeting you scheduled," Toni replies. "What do you want to do?"

I look observantly around the squad room noticing other detectives and patrol officers assigned to the SCS gathering around. "Get everyone ready, Toni; I'll be with Carter in interrogation room one for a while."

"I believe they're called interview rooms, old friend."

Heading off to the holding cells I speak back over my shoulder. "Not today, ma'am."

After retrieving Carter from his cell I shuffle him off into one of our "interrogation" rooms where I have him sit in a chair on one side of the table while I sit across from him slapping down an open file before him displaying the gory pictures of Carmichael's and the Rosenfelts' autopsies.

As I had expected the police officer turned serial killer did not even blink.

"What do these have anything to do with me, Lafayette?" he asks with an undertone of arrogance in his voice. "From what I hear the case has been—how do you put it—solved? At worst I'll just end up in my old cell."

"I don't particularly care about what you heard, Mister Carter. I do, however, care about what you know and what you have done," I reply. "Now, answer my questions to my satisfaction or I will put your head through this table."

Carter stares at me as if I'm a child with a dozen pestering questions. He then chuckles and rolls his eyes. "I'm not obligated to answer you, young blood, especially without my lawyer present. Besides, you've got nothing on me for the Carmichael thing except for being at the wrong place at the right time. So call the state and have me sent back home."

I slip off my sunglasses and lean back in my chair with both of my hands on the table. "I know Xavier put you up to all of this. I'm surprised that he was actually bold enough to contact you himself. But believe you me, my friend, you need to tell me how this is all connected or perhaps there may be someone waiting for you in your cell when you get back there." My tone is evidently effective because the smirk on Carter's face fades away.

"You have no idea what you're in for, no idea at all," Carter says lowly. "You can sit here and threaten me all you want. You'll get your information, but how is it going to help you stay safe? You know as well as I do that Frederick Xavier is a dangerous man, and it doesn't matter how many times you pray or how many friends you have—he will come for you."

I tilt my head while staring Carter down. "He better come for me before I come for him."

"God, you're so self-righteous," Carter replies, adopting his trademark smirk again. "Like I told you before, I was instructed—by Xavier himself—to kill the Rosenfelts. My contact would be Fletcher, who would order the pace of the investigation so that I would be caught when I tied up loose ends. Carmichael was a good guy, but he was paid to spearhead my visitation request. I planted John Xavier's DNA everywhere to try and throw suspicion—but that didn't work to well because you were on the case, and little Xavier became full of himself and overambitious."

Not only does Carter's statement get a rise out of the spirit within me; concerning the little truth he has just revealed Carter himself has taught me all too well the tell-tale markers of lying. In my head I match up Carter's statement from yesterday with what he has just told me, and I find something amiss between the lines.

I stare at Carter with a look of puzzlement, which he notices of course but say nothing in response. He looks at me as if he's expecting me to come to some realization. I stand up and head for the door, refraining from giving away any clues through my facial expressions.

In the squad room again I begin addressing my colleagues concerning the events of the past couple of days. Toni walks up to me before I make it over to my desk, a look of apprehension on her face. The captain will be arriving shortly and the moment we make eye contact it is quite likely that he'll be bringing news of our squad's final duties. Also I will officially be on suspension so I make it my objective to conduct this meeting as fast as possible.

"Ladies and gentlemen, my friends, earlier this week the sheriff's office took over one of our most personal cases. We all know the trials that this squad faces more than any other unit in the department, no one wants us here, and Captain Brooks and Lieutenant Ryan have done all that they can to keep the politics and bureaucracy out of our squad," I exhort. "The order may come down today for our disbandment, but keep doing what you're doing. Save somebody and put the bad guys in jail. Those of us as senior detectives will continue to investigate what we can, but we need your help. If any of you hear anything about the name Frederick Xavier, please let us know. Thank you."

Turning around then I head back over to my desk to retrieve my sidearm from one of the bottom drawers. I notice Toni hanging around behind me as if she were confused or in the least a bit unassuming. "Shouldn't I be rolling with you, Sam," she asks me.

"You're too close to me on this, Toni. I have to do this next bit by myself," I reply softly for reassurance. "I need you to be my eyes and ears here, okay, partner?"

Toni's bright blue eyes convey a sense of concern for me I've never seen before. Although her morals and ethics have always worried me I can perceive that her being around me a lot is starting to change her character.

"Okay, Sam," she answers quietly.

"Okay. Would you have Dawson catch up with that old confidential informant of his and see what the word on the street is? Thank you." I look around the squad room again until I spot Sanz in the crowd and call out to her. I head for the elevator then, with Sanz following close behind me.

Standing in the elevator with Sanz, the doors began to close and the last thing we see of the squad room is Toni waving goodbye and gesturing that the captain is getting off the other elevator.

I smile appreciatively. God is definitely on my side.

With Detective Sanz along for the ride I drop by a local bar and pub aptly named "The Rock-Stop", a place owned and occasionally by Fredrick Xavier himself. I was overly concerned for Sanz's safety, however, so in the car, after turning off the engine, I take time to prep the graceful mother of two.

"Rebecca, I brought you along because we share a kindred spirit and now is not the time for carelessness like that of our partners. We're in the lions' den now."

"I'm more of a veteran at this than you are, *Senor* Lafayette," she admonishes me.

I consider her words respectively. "Okay then. Let's go say hello to evil."

After a hundred years or more of change you would think the atmosphere in a bar would be more hospitable. But that isn't the case with the bars in this country; especially this one, it's filled with cheap cigar and cigarette smoke, beer-slushing and glass clinking, loud music and a couple of men engaging in a loud discussion.

It's not "happy hour" so only a dozen or so brutes occupy the place; one reaches out and pinches Sanz's behind as we head to the bar. Sanz wheels around fist cocked, ready to hit the brute but I stop her and calm her down, pointing her in the direction of the bar. I plant my feet though and drop the brute with a right hook to his jaw.

At the bar Sanz perched herself on a stool, still cooling off from what just happened; I remain standing, requesting of the bar-keeper a few cubes of ice for my hand.

"Sir, has the owner been in here recently?" I ask over the senseless music.

Without speaking, the burly bar-keeper gestures grudgingly toward a booth secluded in the far corner of the room past several pool tables where a couple of heavy-set men were playing pool.

Walking in the given direction I take the lead, not wanting Sanz to be easily noticed by the gentleman sitting down. We approach the booth quietly where none other than Xavier himself was having breakfast with two dark suited gentlemen.

"Well if it isn't Monsieur Lafayette," he says, with a deep rasp in his voice. "I trust you had a safe flight back from Dallas?"

"Fredrick Xavier," I reply soundly as my acknowledgement of him. "I did have a safe flight back in fact, thank you for asking. I cannot say it's nice to see you here though."

"How 'bout that," Xavier says. "I do happen to have offices in many a city though."

"Well, since you're here I can inform you of your son John's death."

Xavier gives me a cold stare. "He was weak and his death was inevitable. His ambition of outdoing me was his downfall. It is only me that can give you a run for your money."

"I doubt you could, sir. But let me change the subject: what do you know about the Rosenfelts' murder—Mark and Gloria Rosenfelt to be exact?"

"Yeah about them—I had heard what happened," Xavier says patting his mouth clean with a napkin. "And I think it's just terrible. How is that Lieutenant Ryan of yours doing by the way?"

"Sir, did you have anything to do with the mayor and his wife's murder?" I ask firmly, staring Xavier down.

"Your tone is accusatorial in nature. And you know better than to ask me that, Lafayette. As a matter of fact, you know better than to accuse me of anything." Xavier returns my stare darkly, which I see out the corner of my eye unsettles Sanz. "You have no proof, and it makes me angry when you accuse me of things without proof—" Xavier feigned a shudder, "makes me want to hurt something—or should I say someone."

Because I've been facing this evil man for so long his subtle tactics do not scare me. In fact it makes me angry.

"You're right, sir, I do know better. So I am going to ask you another accusing question: a man fitting your description was seen visiting Dallas Carter in prison; was that you, sir?"

Xavier's usually content demeanor faded to one of a daring and solemn appearance.

I widen my stance and speak authoritatively to drive my next question home, knowing all too well Xavier's desire to count me among the other dead members of my family. "Why are you here, sir?"

A smirk plays across Xavier's mouth. "I've finally got the time and the resources to close a deal I've been working on for a very long time."

By any other name Xavier's statement was a threat—which I am sure he'll follow through on. So I decide to finish this conversation to go prepare.

"Well I hope the deal is closed on good terms." I turn slowly to leave making sure Sanz behind me.

"It doesn't matter what terms the deal closes on—so as long as it closes," Xavier says wishing us off. "Good day, Detective Lafayette, Detective Sanz."

I mentally give Xavier's points for playing his part of the rather intelligent and deviant crime lord. But I also note my own points for pushing the man's buttons to the extent where I'll know his next move.

Something disturbs me though after my conversation with Xavier…he seems to be more involved in this than I thought he was which doesn't quite work for me.

Our next stop is my brother Duke's office where I usually come to seek more than just brotherly advice. He offers a more in depth perspective on things as a result of his honed legal mind. Sometimes even during the course of every investigation process I make it a point to seek out not only the legal consequences, but also the emotional consequences, all of which Duke has a greater grasp of.

"Duke, this is Detective Rebecca Sanz," I say pointedly, "One of my alternate squad partners."

"Toni introduced us a while ago," Duke replies as matter-of-factly. "But why don't you two have a seat." Duke closes his office door once we're seated before his desk in the guest chairs, and then he comes over to lean against his desk before us.

"Carter's being sent back to prison, Duke, but I know it was him who committed the murders including Carmichael's," I tell him slipping off my sunglasses and messaging my right temple, "I just don't know how I'm going to prove it."

Duke folds his large arms tight against his chest, appearing thoughtful. "I can see your problem: Fletcher's office closed the case and filed it away under its purview so you'll be hard pressed to reopen the whole thing and investigate implications of Fletcher's involvement. Also from what your crime scene investigators have told me the weapon Carter used to kill Carmichael is nowhere to be found."

"Doesn't it bother you guys though how fast this is all going?" Sanz interjects, gesturing towards me. "I mean, since you've been back events following the Rosenfelts' homicide have all been too well orchestrated—to say the least."

Duke looks at me, expectant for some sort of affirmation.

"You are quite right, Rebecca," I say. "Xavier would not be in town if he wasn't initiating some type of master plan."

"What do you suppose it is? I mean someone got some type of benefit from the murders," asks Duke attentively. "But who?"

"I believe it was Fletcher, but I'm not sure. I saw a document on his desk with Xavier's name on it when I visited his office yesterday," I reply.

"That's not much, Samuel," Duke points out. "Just because you saw something doesn't mean it has any validity."

I look up at my brother. "That's why I need you to get me access to Fletcher's office and to Xavier's bar. Perhaps I can find something that will help shed some light on things."

"Sam you and both know that Fletcher has hid those documents somewhere else by now, and you don't have anything for me to take to a judge." Duke shook his head.

"Tell the judge you're concerned about the Sheriff office's handling of recent investigations," I reply. "You'll still be telling the truth."

Duke looks disappointed at me. "My boss and the higher ups will rip me a new one. Not to mention the fact that your squad is already on the chopping block."

Sanz interjects again saying, "Time is against us, but we've always come out on top before."

"This may be it for all of us," I say somberly.

"The future is predicated by the past. So let's ask ourselves—how does Xavier benefit from the Rosenfelts' murders? Through investments? Political or economic influence? A simple message to the rest of us close you?" Sanz points toward me casually. "What motive could Xavier possibly have had to murder the city's mayor? Is it to cause some sort of panic or terror?"

I glance up at Duke who begins to fill Sanz in on our family's relations with the notorious Fredrick Xavier. "First off, Mrs. Sanz, Xavier has been at war with us our family for over fifty years—so he hates us, whatever we try to do, and those who decide to associate themselves with us," he says. "The last living Lafayettes include the two of us, Faith, my wife and two children, and an uncle of ours."

Sanz looks at me in unbelief. "He's killed nearly everyone in your family?"

I only nod an affirmative, not trusting my voice to speak.

"Gentlemen, what if this is an elaborate plot for Xavier to take control over the city? I mean think about it—the city government has been broken for some time now, and without a mayor or lieutenant mayor, the next person in line would be—"

"Roger Camden, senior councilman and lieutenant mayor," Duke says aloud.

A silence issues itself into the room then for a brief moment. I know that Sanz is waiting on my next move, which she does not know will be based on what Duke says next.

"You guys work on finding something that will tie Fletcher and Camden to Xavier; I'll handle our brass," Duke eventually says. "Though I think there'll have to be a hearing on deciding whether or not just to reopen the case."

Sanz stands up slowly and I follow suit. "We can do this," she states.

"I hope you all do be safe out there though," Duke replies sternly.

I follow Sanz to the door telling her to give me a personal moment with Duke and I turn back to my brother after closing the door behind her. "So with Xavier in town, Uncle John isn't too far away."

Duke's expression lightened. "I know. I suspect he'll make himself known after-while."

Our eyes meet in a silent understanding of the necessity of our work—as a team and individuals. Many a time have the two of us been faced with the same obstacles, and to overcome them we've always done what our parents have told us to do since we were kids; and that is work together.

"We have got to stop this man, Samuel," Duke says under his breath.

I slip my sunglasses on slowly and reach for the doorknob. "We will finish what dad started brother."

"My husband and I will be celebrating our twelfth wedding anniversary this saturday," Sanz states as we're heading back to our unmarked squad car. "What about you and Senora Lafayette?"

"Five years next week," I reply opening the driver side door. I add a smile when I continue speaking. "She wanted herself a young buck."

In the car as I start it up my cell phone goes off—which I take out of my pocket to answer. "Lafayette."

"Sam, it's Toni," my old partner says. "Jack just called; he says his informant was picked up by someone in a Sheriff's vehicle. He followed them. Guess where they led him, old friend?"

I cast Sanz a short affirming glance. "To Fletcher?" I question.

"Nope. The Rock-stop."

"Toni, listen carefully. Tell Dawson to back off, tell him to do it now," I reply strictly. "Xavier is there. I repeat: Xavier is there, Toni. He could kill Dawson on sight."

Toni's next response is broken and sparse. "Too late, Sam."

I bite back my tongue from swearing and close my phone, shifting the car into drive… really hard.

No more bloodshed, Lord God, please no more bloodshed.

I haven't even pulled the car to a complete stop in the bar's parking lot before both Sanz and I are jumping out of the car. Together we dash into the bar at the very moment one of Xavier's suits deck Dawson.

Sanz pulls her sidearm and trains it on the man. "Freeze! Police!"

The man looks over at us with a devilish gleam in his eyes then turns back to look at Xavier sitting unperturbed in his favorite booth. It was as if he sought an unspoken command from the crime lord.

This is when I became overly concerned for my partners and myself. I could see out the corner of my left eye several other men in black suits gathering around us looking as if they were about to do harm at the drop of a hat.

I then meet Xavier's dark and wanting stare, deciding for myself what was going to happen next.

"Detective, come over here please," I tell Dawson who was on his knees before his attacker. I raise my hand up to my hip and withdraw my sidearm while keeping my gaze locked on Xavier.

The crime lord kept his expression impassive and casually got up from his table and walked out through the back of the bar.

Now more than ever do I feel like praying. But first I must block one of the suits' wild swings at me—which I am almost too slow to block. But I do punch the man back afterwards, knocking him on his behind, while two other suits tackle me.

Shots fire in the background while I'm on the floor struggling with my attackers, and it does not comfort me, but causes me to realize that one of my partners has been pressed into discharging their weapon.

I throw one of the suits off of me and punch the other until he's unconscious. Then I get up to spot Sanz and Dawson; the former was cuffing two men whom she had shot in the legs, the latter was banging another suit's head on the bar-counter.

The suit I had pushed away was back up now and he grabbed me from behind, pinning my arms behind my back. As I struggled, another suit was sneaking up on Dawson and I was unable to break free to stop him.

"Jack, behind you!" I shout. I break my second attacker's hold on me and force-fully connect my elbow to his rib cage and then close-line him, laying him out. I quickly look for my sidearm on the floor—which I find and pick up.

Another gunshot rings out just before I turn around. Facing the action again I spot Dawson still struggling with the man I had warned him about, but I aim my gun at the man who was holding Sanz hostage, a gun pressed to the side of her head.

"Let her go," I order the man sternly without raising my voice. "Or else…" I slip off my sunglasses and toss them to the floor, using both of my hands to train my weapon on him for emphasis.

"You drop your gun first," the man replies pressing the gun into Sanz's temple.

Instantly I see fear in the woman's eyes as she looks expectantly at me. Something tells me that it's not her time to leave this world and that she knows it—which was why she came to fix me with such an expectant look in the first place.

"Sir, let her go. Now," I say again, not letting Dawson's desperate struggle in the background distract me.

"You're not going to shoot through her. You put your gun down," the man replies.

"Shoot him, Lafayette!" Dawson shouts.

I did have a partial opening to shoot but it was not the right second to make my move. I exchange a mutual look of penitence with her—which brings us both to the same understanding of the consequences if I miss the bad guy.

"Lafayette, kill him!"

"Jack, be quiet!" I tell Dawson. I address the suit again saying, "Sir, I warn you again: let her go."

"Let her go you say? Okay." The man moves his finger to take his shot.

However, I'm the faster, and I manage to hit the man with the clean shot I had of his shoulder. He went down and Sanz slumped to her knees, petrified. Dawson finally takes out his attacker at the same time I come to stand over the downed suit whose gun I kick from his reach.

Sanz is shaking from aftershock, holding herself. I keep my sidearm trained on the man I shot while hunching down to Sanz's side to wrap my arm around her.

"You're okay now, Rebecca. It's over." I cast Dawson an angry glare. "Everything's going to be alright."

LAFAYETTE

Catching Dawson off his guard in the locker room I grab him and jack him up against his locker door, slamming it shut, and getting in his face for emphasis while I spoke. "What the devil is your problem, Jack?" I begin to fume. "You almost got me, Rebecca, and yourself killed out there."

"Look man, I'm sorry. But I saw an opportunity so I took it. Any good officer would have done the same."

I jack Dawson up higher. "Not me, Jack. I would have done only what I was told."

"Oh please, don't play that 'I'm holier than thou' crap with me," he says struggling against my grip. "You'd get down just like the rest of us if you weren't so self-righteous."

"I behave this way because I know that every action I take has a consequence," I reply strongly. "Now if we are going to work together you are going to have to listen to me and the others—and not just for our sakes either but for yours. Do you understand?"

Dawson turns his head to look away—as if that would make me go away.

"Do you understand, Jack?" I ask again sterner than before.

"Yes. I do," Dawson answers; his voice breeding with contempt.

I slowly release the man, wary in case he planned on hitting me, but offering him a nod of satisfaction.

I do sympathize with him because I used to identify with him when I was a teenager—always making the worst of choices, if not directly. However since then I have become a better person, a better man of God.

"We are strong men, peace keepers, Jack, with female partners; you must be more responsible than what you've shown yourself to be today."

"I'll try—"

"No, don't try. Just do, my friend. Just do your very best."

After leaving Dawson in the locker room I made my way up to the squad room via one of the elevators on the main floor. As I step off the elevator into the squad room Sanz steps pass me onto the elevator carrying her work duffel bag and looking tired.

"Rebecca, I thought you already left?" I say to her, curious. "Are you really okay?"

"I'm fine, Senor Lafayette. But I'm heading home to rest now," Sanz replies softly. "After all these years the job still gets to me."

"You wouldn't be human if it didn't. But do get home safely. Oh, and if you find yourself ever in the financial district drop by Milan-Lafayette, whatever you order is on the house, just say I sent you."

Sanz gives me a kind and lovely smile. "Thank you."

I step back to allow the elevator doors to close, offering a final goodbye wave.

"Sam, in my office now," Captain Brooks calls from his office door.

With my only connection to a better spirit safely enclosed in the elevator, I sigh and turn to parade into Brooks' office. The captain closes the door once I'm inside and heads over to stand behind his desk with a grim expression on his face. I stand quietly before him, fiddling with my sunglasses in my hands.

"Sam, I'm sorry but it's over. I've been instructed to relieve you of duty," Brooks informs me. "And the others have been instructed to cease working on your cases."

"On what grounds?" I ask lowly.

"Misconduct of investigations."

"Well you know that's lie. We're so close to the truth and they're trying to stop me, trying to stop us." I look the older man squarely in the eyes. "Jack's only informant was picked up by Fletcher and was taken to Xavier's bar. Dawson found that extremely telling, and I agree with him."

"That doesn't matter anymore, Sam. The Rosenfelts' case has been closed and that's that."

I step closer to the desk. "You know as well as I do that this case isn't closed."

"Can you say with certainty that Fletcher was there?" Brooks asked.

I look away despondently and answer with a low tone, "No."

"I'm sorry but we have to follow protocol. We can't do anything more at this point, not without giving HQ any more reason to hang us. Now, Sam, please…"

"This is not sitting well with me, old friend." I pull my badge and my sidearm from my belt and lay them on the desk. "And you're lying; *we* can't do anything about this but a detective with a captain's position like yourself can." I slip my sunglasses back on and head for the door quickly.

"Uneasy lies the head that wears the crown, Sam," Brooks says just before I step out of sight.

I went out into the parking lot afterwards and cross it to head for my wife's car, however I spot all three of my partners hanging around the car, looking all but out of it. I look toward Toni first. "Ma'am?"

"While you and Rebecca here were out, we had a uniform officer search the phone records of a certain payphone near Xavier's bar, the only payphone within fifty miles by the way, and guess what they found?" Toni says smiling.

I glance over at Sanz and Dawson who also were smiling as if they were children with candy. "A history of calls from it to some sort of phone under Xavier's name?" I answer Toni.

"Better: to a city work phone connected to Fletcher's office. And guess what else. Willard Devlin was indeed just an alias. Frederick Xavier just used that name to avoid being noticed," Toni explains.

"That means, Carmichael was in on it and was taken out because he was a loose end."

Toni answers, "Yep."

"And as far as we know the sheriff's office didn't question Carter about it," Dawson adds.

"I think we already know our next move but I do believe if you have anything to say, Sam, now would be the time," Toni says standing tall.

Her new righteous demeanor catches me off guard but nonetheless inspires pride in my heart. All of my doubt of her growth as a woman of principle found itself recanted, and as I see her proudly flanked by the others I understand now that I am most assuredly not alone in the fight against evil.

I glance up at the window of the captain's office and as I expected, found Brooks peering out of it, a cautious look on his face.

"Didn't the captain tell you guys I'm on suspension and that you are to leave this case alone?" I ask still looking up.

"He said something about the squad being disbanded," Dawson replies, "but I didn't hear anything about suspension."

"Well, in any case you know now that I can't lead you guys, officially?"

"We won't tell if you don't," Sanz says.

I look over my fellow detectives studiously. "This could get ugly," I tell them.

"Like it hasn't already?" Toni shrugs.

"You're right." I raise my head to glance at Brooks in the window again. "From here on in we can't trust anyone except each other."

"Not even the captain?" Toni asks, doubtful.

"He needs plausible deniability," I reply sorely. I look at the others again. "Meet me at Duke's office tonight at eight-thirty and we'll proceed from there."

"Got it," Toni replied. She and the others left separately then; making sure to give me a curt nods of acknowledgement before getting in their cars and driving off.

I'm left standing in place however, looking up at Brooks, who had a gleam in his eye I've never seen before. He then glances pointedly up at the sky, which I focus my attention on. The sky was noticeably clouding over. I look again and Brooks had disappeared from view.

Get going... my conscience tells me. I ignored it though to stand a minute longer while in the increasing sprinkling showers. The way the first drop of rain rolls down my face rejuvenated my soul in a way I couldn't explain.

That's another one of someone's mysterious ways…

It wasn't long until I found myself staring at my after school center for youths. Granted it was now raining harder than it did when I was back at the station, and I had no business standing outside of my wife's car in the thick of it. However, I just had to get one last look at the building before construction crews came to remodel it this coming monday.

If one truly knew me though, you'd know I would be lying if I said I wasn't wondering myself crazy over how my vision for the future of the city's youths was tarnished while I left it in the care of others. The building before me stood for nearly everything I believed in. I wanted the city's youth to see that a man of faith did more than just shout from a pulpit or through a blow horn, but rather became personally involve with making change.

Whether by counseling, preaching, or leading by example, I believe it was way past time to make a change in the way we live and how we act toward one another.

I smile at that idea, and feeling as if I was seeing with new eyes again, I look at the youth center I established before me and envisioned it being swarmed by young people that were interested as I am in making a difference.

Rolling down my cheeks now weren't only water droplets but tears of joy, in response to the vision God was obviously showing me. I saw children; even my own children, doing what the Lord wanted us to do, using faith and fellowship.

Thank you, Lord.

Just then, the spirit brought something to my remembrance: I was supposed to be picking my wife Faith up early from work in a few minutes. And that is when I get on my way.

I open the door and climb in behind the steering wheel, starting the car; it's not long before I'm on the road headed toward my wife's restaurant. Because of the rain though, the streets were becoming increasingly difficult to navigate, both the ditches and the roadways flooding over.

Passing through a green light, I could tell that the minivan in front of me was starting to hydroplane, just as a long-bed pickup truck went speeding past my car. Those actions, combined with the fact that there was a bend coming up ahead in the road, was not the best of unfolding circumstances.

I speed up and maneuvered my car to where I was hogging both lanes; I did this so that the drivers behind me wouldn't get caught up in the accident that I was sure was about to happen.

Just as we were all approaching the curve in the road, an average sedan in one of the opposite lanes came fishtailing into the pickup truck's lane, ramming it nearly head-on. The truck, however, collided backwards into the minivan, knocking it completely off the road and into a ditch while the truck and sedan came to a stop on the shoulder of the road.

I could hardly comprehend what had happened. The severity of the accident stunned me. The driver of the truck had been thrown from his truck out the passenger side and was now laying on the ground twenty feet away; the sedan's front end had been so badly smashed that it was now part of the truck's engine, all fixed in a twisted arraignment of metal; but it was what happened to the minivan that had me jumping out of my car and rushing over toward the scene, using my cell to call in to dispatch for paramedics and other aid. For some reason the Spirit told me not to worry about whoever was in the sedan.

The minivan had flipped three times before coming to rest upside down in the ditch alongside the road. Water was rising fast because of the rain, which threatened to submerge the whole vehicle. But I climbed down anyway to the minivan to see if I could help anyone that might be hurt; ignoring the fact the water level was now at my ankles.

Two young girls were climbing out through the broken windshield and driver's side window, crying and screaming, all the while a man—obviously their father—were struggling to breathe because the van was leaning on half of his body, particularly his torso. He had obviously been thrown from the vehicle finding him under it when it came to a rest. The fact that the increasing water levels was about to drown him made his situation that much worse.

"Save him, save him, save daddy!" the young girls cried when they noticed me.

"Okay, okay, I will; I'm a policeman, okay, and what I need you to do is go back there to my car, okay?" I tell the young girls, taking off my suit jacket. "Here take my jacket to cover you. My car's right up there; you two hurry and get inside."

I watched them go off to my car, making sure they were okay before I turned back toward their father and his predicament. I was at his side, gripping his free hand with one of my own when he looked up at me in the near beating rain saying, "My girls—save my girls."

"They're okay, I'm gonna get you out of here." I move to push the minivan, but my effort to rock the vehicle off of the man is quickly met with resistance. I try again, and again, a total of four times before I fall back onto the slope of ground behind me.

"Oh, no you don't. Don't you give up like that, not here, not now," I warn him.

My clothes now thoroughly soaked by the rain, weighed me down in my resumed efforts to save the man trapped beneath his minivan. I stood up and threw my weight against the vehicle twice, noticing it budge a little. The man cried out in pain. Thunder began to rumble across the sky then, which meant that our situation would only get worse because of more drenching rain. I already couldn't believe it was raining so hard, the raindrops felt like needles against my skin.

"This is going to hurt me a lot more than it's going to hurt you, my friend," I warn the man. He held his breath as the water levels rose above his head. Meanwhile, I braced my back against the ground's inclined slope behind me and pressed my feet up to the side of the minivan. I used all of my strength and then some to push and rock the vehicle off of the man's body. I could feel the muscles in my back straining under the pressure; a muscle in both my left arm and right leg were even pulled past the tension point, and I cried out in pain. A lightning bolt struck a power transformer up the roadway then, leaving a loud booming sound over the air.

Remarkably, I held the minivan up just long enough for the man to crawl out of from underneath it in the water. After he was free, I immediately went limp and dropped the vehicle, falling back on the sloped ground again. There I lied, on my back on the ground, in the rain, with the sirens of ambulances and other emergency crews blaring over the air.

For helping me to save one more person, I thanked my God above.

Later, I found myself carefully sitting down to one of the private tables in Faith's restaurant, I found it amazing how quickly my body had begun to heal after saving a man from being crushed beneath his vehicle. My father used to tell me when I was little that God takes care of those who suffer for him—even physically. And you know what? Daddy was right.

"Come here often?" Faith asks slipping herself into the chair on the other side of the table.

I smile shyly, glancing around at the various patrons occupying the restaurant, attempting to dine out for the evening. Looking back across the table however, I lock gazes with Faith, feeling a little more embarrassed.

Something in her eyes tells me she wants to play—not a first I might add, since we've been married for a little while now.

"I'm looking for my wife—the owner," I reply absently. "Have you seen her?"

"I think I have," Faith says grinning, looking around. "Does she have shoulder-length black hair, a cute little dimply smile, and satiny mocha skin?"

It takes me great effort to keep from grinning as I reply, "Yes, ma'am, she does."

"Does she also get picked up sometimes after work by a tall, dark, and handsome man?"

"Yes, ma'am."

Faith broadens her impish grin. "I'm going to trip you up one day sweetheart; you're too good at thinking on your feet."

I stare wonderingly into her eyes. "Maybe," I reply. "You ready to go home?"

"Yeah, I can't wait—"

Explosive gunshots suddenly begin blasting through the windows into the diner and I tackle Faith down onto the floor out of harm's way while shouting to everyone else, "Everybody get down!"

The gunshots continued blowing through the place, and every time I rose my head up I could see debris flying everywhere and one or two people falling down gruesomely. Chaos took over the place, people were screaming, and ear-shattering explosions echoed over and over again.

Covering my wife Faith with my body I noticed she was whimpering and shaking with fear; that alone made me angry at whoever was shooting.

The shooting stopped as abruptly as it had started, with someone shouting loud enough for me to hear afterwards.

"Xavier sends his regards, Lafayette!"

LAFAYETTE

"How Did I let this happen?" I ask no one particular leaning against the file cabinet in my brother's office. "Of all the ways to come at me? I will hunt Xavier down for this."

"How's Faith doing, Samuel?" Duke wisely interjects. I stand up straight and turn toward him, who was sitting in his chair behind his desk.

I could see that everyone was following me with troubled eyes as I moved about, but that didn't concern me. My concern was focusing on how I could get Frederick Xavier back for what he did to my wife's restaurant. Rest assured I was going to make him pay for what he did. Since he was bold enough to have one of his henchmen to commit such a terrible act, I will be bold enough to take the fight to him.

"She was shaken up pretty bad so I took her home and put her to bed as soon as Ryan and emergency crews showed up," I say, gesturing emphatically with my hands.

"You should be home with her, comforting her, Sam," Rebecca tells me, sitting in one of the guest chairs in front of the desk.

"I couldn't agree more, Rebecca, but I'm here now and I want to knock some heads for this."

"How many people were hurt, Sam?" Toni asks me, also sitting in one of the guest chairs in front of the desk.

"Ten with minor injuries, five were shot and killed, and there's a little boy fighting for his life right now after taking a shot to the head," I reply bleakly.

"That's just sick," Jack says, perched on the edge of Duke's desk.

"My God," Rebecca voices.

I nod affirmatively and turn back to Duke. "The audacity to have someone shoot up a public place. That was an outright display of violence just to send me a message," I tell him. "He's changed the rules again. This game of his is becoming too dangerous to play."

"Indeed," Duke replies, appearing thoughtful. "This is worse than when it first began."

Rebecca stood up then and came over to me, a motherly gleam in her eyes as she spoke. "My friend, you should go home to your wife and keep her company."

I started to voice my protest but Duke out spoke me saying, "She's right, Samuel, you need to take a step back for the time being. We can handle it."

"What about the search warrants?" I ask.

"My superiors have been giving me the run around and all the judges except for one won't even agree to hear my case. I barely managed to get a hearing scheduled with this particular judge on Friday," Duke explains.

I look to Toni for her input. "We won't serve any warrant without you, Sam. Go on home to Faith; we'll help Ryan search for whoever shot up the restaurant in the meantime."

My brother and my friends care for me well and they speak the truth: I need to go home.

It's ten o'clock when I finally get back home and stepping in the door I spot Faith curled up on the sofa, the TV's flickering light flooding the room. I made it a point to approach cautiously: not wishing to wake or startle her, though I distinctly recall placing her in the bed earlier.

"Don't worry about waking me, Sam," Faith says out of the blue. "I can't sleep tonight."

"You'll fall asleep, trust me." I take off my suit jacket and slip out of my shoes, tossing the former onto the chair off to the side.

Faith moves over on the couch to allow me room to sit. Then she cuddled up next to me, resting her head on my shoulder while I wrapped my arm around her waist to hold her close.

"I thought you were going after the bad guys?" Faith says, after a while of me stroking her side.

"Our allies decided to hold off on that for tonight," I reply taking my finger and curling stray tresses of her hair back behind her ears.

"In other words they said for you to go home and rest?"

"We have very caring friends."

"They really do care about you Sam."

I chuckle. "Not as much as you. But let me ask you this, how are you feeling after today?"

"Angry, confused, sad—and scared," Faith says. "I've never been so scared in my life until today. I was a cop for almost eleven years, I was shot, blown up, ran over, and I suffer from multiple-sclerosis.

But they killed people, Sam…at my restaurant, my place of peace. Yet, never mind what could have happened to me, but what if you had been killed? Regardless of the resolve I had when we were both wearing the badge—that was different. What if I had lost you today?"

"I can't imagine the hurt that would have put you through sweetheart."

"That's what I'm afraid of, Sam. What will I do if something happens to you?" The sincerity in Faith's voice disturbs me because I know where it's coming from; I felt the same way when she was a detective and out in the field with me. I still feel the same way.

"You'll have to find a way to go on, Faith. If I lost you I would be a very broken man, but I would push my way on because I know that's what you would want for me. I appreciate that about you more than anything—your desire is to see that I make it, that I'll be okay," I answered solemnly. "Likewise that's what I would expect of you. We're in this together, but if one of us can't go any further than the one remaining has to keep the legacy, the faith alive."

Faith tilts her head back, her eyes becoming teary. "I want both of us to make it, Sam."

"We will." I lean closer to Faith and kiss her forehead gently. "We have miles to go before we sleep."

LAFAYETTE

For the past half hour I have been staring at Christopher Russell. Mr. Russell was the gentleman whom I pulled from the car accident the day before. You could hardly tell from seeing him lay in his hospitable bed that the man was somewhat tall, about six-foot-three or so. He was bandaged up pretty good; his right leg was in a cast, a brace was around his neck, and both his arms were wrapped in some type of white, covering. Looking at his face, it was easy to note the numerous stitches across his forehead.

That's when I thought to myself, there have been one too many times where I have been in his same position. Regardless of the fact my injuries have always come as a result of doing my job, I could not help but worry about the day no one will be able to save me like the way I saved Mr. Russell. Living forever is not a goal of mine, but by God's grace it has always been my hope to transition into the next life when I'm very old and very grey.

I don't want to leave an incomplete life. I don't want to go out on the job. However, the one reoccurring dream that I have always had places me in a situation where I have saved everyone except myself. I have never questioned why I am who I am or why I must do what I do, but my reality has become very real as of late. I may not make it out of this alive.

Mr. Russell groans as he awakens, struggling to shift his position in his bed. This stirs my attention and focus from my thoughts to observing Russell more closely. "Good afternoon, Mr. Russell," I say softly.

"You look familiar, who are you?" Russell asks with a raspy voice.

I stand up from sitting in the chair by the bedside. "My name is Samuel Lafayette. You were in a car accident yesterday with your daughters and I pulled you from it. Don't worry; your girls are safe. They're downstairs with their mother."

Russell gives a sigh of relief. "Thank you."

"Mr. Russell, I hear that you're a private investigator and that you just solved a really big case."

"I guess," Russell scoffs. "I could have handled it better. I could have celebrated at home; we were just leaving from getting ice cream when we had the accident."

"Well now you can celebrate again since you all made it through the accident alright." I start moving toward the end of the bed, taking my sunglasses out of my suit pocket.

"I suppose you're right. We should cherish every moment of life because of how fragile it is."

Russell closes his eyes so he doesn't see me pause and stare at him one last time in wonder. "Thank you for that, Mr. Russell."

Russell opens his eyes and looks back at me with an understanding in his gaze that I recognize. In that moment I can tell of the mutual and universal respect we both share, knowing nothing more about each other than our names. I slip my sunglasses on and Russell nods in my direction.

"Keep making a difference, Samuel," Russell says.

"You do the same, Christopher," I reply.

Since I was no longer officially on duty I found myself with enough time to make rounds of visiting the few friends I have. I knocked on Mack Ryan's office door to get his attention before I entered. Making it a point to observe his demeanor and appearance before I made myself at home in his new office.

"It's good to see you, Sam," Ryan says, leaning back against his desk. His jeans, untucked, white button-down shirt and dark blue blazer let me know that he's been busy getting settled into the office.

I ease down into one of the gust chairs, unbuttoning my black suit jacket. "So you're the new squad commander of homicide," I say nonchalantly.

"Co-commander," Ryan replies. "I and another lieutenant answer to the assistant chief of detectives."

"Two days and they already have you transferred and commanding another post." I shake my head slowly. They respect you only because of the loss of your brother. One could say that's their heart eating away at them."

Ryan folds his arms against his chest. "Careful, Sam, you wouldn't want to say that too loud."

I scoff.

"I think they moved me because there's something bad about to happen to Serial Crime. They want it shut down bad. I got a call from the assistant chief of detectives this morning wanting me to know that my people will be taking over all of Serial Crime's active cases."

"No way," I say aloud.

"I also had a visit this morning from Sheriff Fletcher and Mayor-Elect Roger Camden. The purpose of said visit was to assure me that they had my back and that they're extremely sorry for my brother's death."

"This is bad, Mack, this is very bad."

"I know. The powers-that-be are handing down reports and whatnot instructing us to relax our patrols in certain areas of the city. I can't express enough how aggravated I am about all of this. I want these evil bastards to pay, Sam; I want them to pay soon."

Hearing the pain in Ryan's voice, I lower my head. I had been praying since the start of everything for Ryan's peace of mind. What I did not know until now is the deep-ridden angst he was harboring. Revenge was eating away at him. He knew as well as I did the lengths evil people like Frederick Xavier would go to, just to win. Fletcher and Camden seemed to be Xavier's two main knights and the governing police administration seemed to be his throne.

What Ryan did not know however, was how much I related to his internal pains. "My friend, it would appear that everyone else is either too afraid or have their hands tied. So it's up to you and I to finish this."

"Jacob won't help?" Ryan asks.

"He retires soon. Jeopardizing his benefits and all would undermine our collective initiative, because you know that's what they'll go after first," I reply. "This is war now."

LAFAYETTE

It's very early friday morning when I push open the doors of the church and step inside; five thirty in the morning to be exact. I start slowly down the aisle for the altar, hoping to voice my feelings to the Lord.

Pastor Anderson usually leaves the door open for stragglers and people like me, hoping to have quite time with God; and I make a mental note to thank him for not ceasing the habit.

However, I find my heart extremely heavy with the week coming to a close. Since I've been back, I've killed someone who was a friend-turned-enemy; my job has been suspended as a form of retribution; my wife's life has been jeopardized by the destruction of her restaurant; and now, if the bad guys continue to have their way the city will be lost.

"This must be a test of my faith—our faith. How could it not be?" I ask, approaching the altar, and slipping off my sunglasses. Before the indescribable aura over the pulpit again, I bow, laying my sunglasses on the floor beside me.

Either I am going to save this city or die trying. Yet, I feel, every time that I think about it, the latter will be the case. I know the Lord's ways are not for me to search or know but I cannot help but to wonder how much better things would go for me if I were more enlightened.

Are you there, Lord? It's such a silly question to ask, but sometimes when you go through trials and tests you can't help but to ask. You think that there's no way God can be present and allow bad things to happen. If I had not known who or what God is to me then I would not believe in grace or furthermore deliverance.

It is in moments of silence like this that I hear God speak to me, and that he did before I even asked my silly question. I would not be here today if not for God working through the tests and trials of my faith to deliver me. I remind myself that this trouble that I'm in right now, this trouble that my friends and I find ourselves in will not last always. We must fight; we must contend against the evil that we are finding in these high places.

We will be the difference; we will win.

I stand up, wiping the single tear that found itself rolling down my cheek, and slipped on my sunglasses. I button the jacket of my gray, three-piece suit, and head toward the door of the church, when suddenly my cell phone rings.

"Lafayette," I answer, slipping the phone out of my pocket and up to my ear.

"Sam, you won't believe what just happened," Toni's voice breaks the silent air through the phone.

"No suspense, Toni."

"Dallas Carter just escaped prison."

"Your honor, how can the people of this city trust our law enforcement agencies when those agencies do not even trust another?!" my brother Duke says before the taciturn-looking judge sitting behind the bench. My brother reminds me of a large and irate bear as he roars his case in the middle of the court room. It's not a trial being heard today but a hearing on whether or not the Sheriff's office handled the homicide investigation into the Rosenfelts' murder appropriately, and though my brother is doing a great job pleading the facts, the sheriff and his office's legal counsel is fighting back hard.

"Your honor," Sheriff Fletcher begins. "Mr. Lafayette here is trying to reopen a case on the suspicion I had something to do with it, nothing more nothing less."

I chuckle at Fletcher's statement and what Jack Dawson says sitting beside me in the back of the courtroom along with Toni and Rebecca.

"You had a lot to do with it, Mr. Fletcher," Jack murmurs.

"Mr. Lafayette, do you have any substantial evidence linking the sheriff to the man whom you say actually murdered the Rosenfelts?" the judge asks.

Duke sighs. "Not at hand, sir. The detectives who were originally investigating that avenue were either reassigned or suspended. But might I add that those facts alone point to something akin to a cover-up."

"No, Mr. Lafayette it points to corrective action within the police department and an over-reach of your authority as an assistant district prosecutor," the judge says. "I note the presence of both your boss and the District Attorney."

"Your honor, I have witnesses who can provide testimony concerning expedited requests of DNA evidence, the falsification of internal reports, and sightings of Sheriff Fletcher with known drug and weapons trafficker Frederick Xavier," Duke lowers his voice.

"It is apparent, your honor, that Mr. Lafayette has an agenda here," Fletcher's lawyer states. "If one was to connect the dots, they could see that Mr. Lafayette is acting on behalf of the police department's disbanded notorious Serial Crime Squad. A squad that has cost this city hundreds of thousands of dollars in property damage as a result of its investigations. In addition to employing Mr. Lafayette's brother, the ever rebellious Samuel Xavier."

The courtroom fell silent then as the few people inside the room turned to look at Duke and the lowly expressions his demeanor made. I felt my brother's pain over the legal beating he was taking. He glanced in my direction with strained eyes. I wanted nothing more than to clear the distance between me and Fletcher and beat the living crap out of him—but I kept myself restrained.

"Your honor, it does not escape me how truthful that perception may look. However, you must consider how you would act if you knew your peers were out to strip you of your reputation and your livelihood in order to cover up a murder that they committed," Duke explains. "I may not have a job at the end of the day, but I came in here your honor with a purpose, especially after receiving information of Dallas Carter's escape from prison and information that Mr. Carter has been operating out of a house that belongs to Sheriff Fletcher's wife. Now, if I'm not mistaken, Sheriff Fletcher and his wife are estranged, but as of late she has been receiving large sums of money from Sheriff Fletcher that his annual salary cannot account for."

"Your honor, my financials are private information," Fletcher said aloud.

The judge looks at Fletcher accusingly. "Mr. Fletcher, your salary is a matter of public record and if I'm hearing Mr. Lafayette correctly, your wife has agreed to testify against you," he says. "As such I perceive collusion from your party."

"Your honor, we request that the sheriff be relieved of duty and his office turn the files of the investigation into the Rosenfelts' murder over to Lieutenant Mack Ryan and his squad," Duke says righteously.

"I will answer your request, Mr. Lafayette, but by no means does this address the police department's internal matter of the Serial Crime Squad's future. In addition, search warrants will be issued for the respective locations submitted to the court on this matter and my office will be filing motions with the state for oversight into the District Attorney's office on the suspicion of misconduct and maleficence. Case proceedings will begin immediately following jury selection." The judge took his gavel and banged it determinately. The subsequent outbursts that followed were difficult to distinguish from being either for or against the judge's decision.

It is absolutely the sweetest thing to my ears.

"We won this round," Duke says meeting us in the back of the courtroom. He and I look on proudly, seeing the bailiff take the sheriff away into custody.

Noticing my partners flanking me I slip on my sunglasses saying, "And we'll win the next too."

"Carter, open up, it's the police!" Toni says aloud. I'm standing beside her outside the front door of Elizabeth Fletcher's house. With us are Jack, Rebecca, Ryan and his squad's tactical unit.

Now I'm not supposed to be here but with so much riding on this I decided to tag along with the others—all of which had been waiting in the same position outside and around the house for the last ten minutes.

I signal to Toni that he's not coming out and that I smell decomposed flesh from inside. As an acknowledgement she nods. I then move aside to let Jack closer to the door, and I head over to the end of the porch where I jump over the side and take up position with three members of the tactical unit in the drive way.

Looking back I wait for Toni's signal to proceed—which she gives, sending my party and me up the driveway to the garage; hearing Jack kick in the door and Toni shouting commands.

"Get the lock, gentlemen," I tell the tactical members once we reach the garage door. They indeed take care of the lock with bolt cutters and we move strategically inside, although I'm the only one without a weapon.

No one's inside so we begin looking around the place—which is littered with empty cans, of all kinds, turned over workstations, bawled up paper, candy wrappers and a loud ticking sound. My search for the sound leads me to the far side of the garage where an upside-down trash can was behind a bicycle. I push the bike out of the way and lift the trash can slowly. I find several sticks of active dynamite attached to a timer.

This is crazy.

"Gentlemen, back out the way we came, right now!"

The tactical team outran me on our way out of the garage and when I'm barely half way down the driveway the garage explodes with an ear-shattering boom, the blast knocking me to the ground, with a sheering force.

"Sam!" Toni calls, once the explosion died down.

My partners came running up the drive to my side, to help me up, and though it hurt seriously I managed to roll myself over and sit up on the ground, coughing from the charged dust and smoke.

"Sam, are you okay?" Toni asks overly concerned.

I look up at her. "I'm not as fast as I used to be," I say, reaching up for her to help me onto my feet and *we* walk/limp back down the drive.

"What's the scene inside?" I ask taking off my tactical vest.

"There's a decomposed male body inside—not Carter's, and it looks as if he's left town. It's trashed in there, my friend," Toni replies as we made it to our unmarked squad cars parked in front of the house. "We also found a stash of weapons and a prepaid cell. The call log's filled with calls to the same number associated with Fletcher's work phone."

Jack hands me a piece of a paper looking like it's been printed on. "What do you think, Lafayette? Looks like part of a reservation for an airplane ticket," he says.

I reach in through the window of my car and get my cell phone off the dash. "That guy in there was sent to kill Carter," I tell the others.

"He didn't do a very good job," Rebecca quips, receiving an admiring glance from Jack.

I use my cell to make a call while listening to the others piece together what I already know.

"Xavier sent after Carter cause he thought he was more liable than Fletcher to turn on him," Toni says, "Which he is."

"But Carter must've thought he could just leave and Xavier would forget about him," Rebecca says. "I don't see how Carter was that fearful of him though."

"Xavier's cutting all ties to himself before they lead Sam's brother to him," Jack puts in, "So somehow both Xavier and Carter heard what went down in the courtroom today."

"What about Camden?" Rebecca voiced.

"That's between Sam and Duke," Toni replies.

"We're in the last stretch now alright." Jack is the first to pay attention when I close my phone. I look from him to the others.

"Carter's at the airport trying to get on a flight to San Diego," I inform them.

"Just as we expected," Toni says.

"And there's four armed men chasing after him," I say pointedly. "Airport security can't handle what's going there either."

Jack pops his knuckles pointedly, saying, "You still ready to knock some heads, Lafayette?"

I pull our unmarked car to a stop before the entrance of the city's airport and get out, along with Toni; Jack and Rebecca parked right behind us and got out, followed by Ryan and his squad's tactical unit.

I met Toni at the trunk of our unmarked car, taking off my damaged Kevlar vest and setting it in the trunk. I push a spare Kevlar vest to the side and pick up a standard issue sidearm from the gear rack. Toni notices and reaches past me for the spare Kevlar vest, handing it toward me.

"Um, no sir—you put this on. We're not taking any chances," she states.

"I know it is protocol, but I hate those things," I reply.

"One just saved your life from an explosion back at the house, Sam." Toni shoves the vest at me harder. "So put it on."

I take the vest from her, with a smirk in response to her concerned behavior. As I strap the vest on, Toni pulls a shotgun from the gear rack in the trunk and ammunition for it. She loads the shotgun with the ammunition and expressively pumps it with one hand.

"Showoff," I tell her.

"Boy, I am glad to see you guys here," shouts a stout, balding man in an airport security uniform running up to our group. "It's crazy in there. We're shutting down the airport now. They're shooting around bystanders."

I close the trunk and turned toward the man, noting Ryan and his tactical officers—who were in full tactical uniform—joining us. "We'll get a handle on the situation now, sir. Just continue clearing all terminals near their location and then back away."

Toni turns toward everyone and says, "Everyone, listen, there are four very dangerous men inside and a well-trained former police officer—who will kill, I repeat kill anyone who will attempt to stop them. Don't be a hero, if they try to advance on you call for back up."

Everyone disperses and head inside quickly, Toni and I being among the last after I step up onto the curb.

"That goes for you as well, Sam. Don't go off own your own. I couldn't bear telling Faith if something bad happened to you," Toni tells me as we head inside.

"Don't worry about me, old friend. I always have backup," I reply, before heading on inside.

Jack and I paired up as we ran through the airport terminals looking for the armed gunmen. I let Jack take the lead since I was not cleared for duty. With me even being involved, we all knew that reprimands would be handed down on all of us; probably for more than just my involvement. Additional things such as operating without our commanding officer's knowledge/consent and executing warrants outside of our squad's purview could all bring about hefty penalties for my partners and me. Not to mention the headache Mack Ryan will have when the brass questions him; being the senior officer on site. However, none of that matter. You could read it on our facial expressions and in our actions; we were going to protect and serve.

Toni and Rebecca had went off on their own to help corner one of the suits that was chasing Dallas Carter, and it was my hope they didn't have to fight any of the suits. The reason being is if the men chasing Carter do indeed work for Frederick Xavier then they would be very skilled in the martial arts like Xavier himself. The whole idea reminded me of the situation earlier in the week at Xavier's bar which we almost did not make it out of.

"Jack," I say with the intent of directing him to an open service door ahead. The door was situated just before a restroom lounge; but I think twice about it. It was too apparent a place to be for a gunman, but I just could not pass it up without checking it out.

"Never mind, you guys go on," I tell him and the security guard that had following along with us. They keep going while I walk through the open door, alone.

Gripping my sidearm firmly, I use my acute senses to help warn and guide me as I make my way down a well-lighted stairwell.

Twenty heartbeats later I'm at the bottom, which opens up to employee parking grounds. I slowly step down from the last step, however, hearing heavy breathing around the corner.

Dallas Carter comes around the corner swinging wildly with a lead pipe, knocking my weapon from my hand, but missing my head. I duck and punch him in his side failing to avoid his back swing, which knocks me down on my back.

He moves to kick me while I'm down but I wrap my legs around his ankle and use enough force to make him fall. He tries to swing at my side with the lead pipe again but I roll to my knees and hit him in the throat. Then I punch him and lay him out on his back on the ground.

"Let me get this straight," I begin, taking off my sunglasses and standing over Carter, kicking the lead pipe from his hand. "Xavier helps you escape the first time to kill the mayor and his wife, you kill the middleman Carmichael. Then after you're caught, Fletcher helps you escape again as some type of payment for your services but Xavier also sends his henchman after you so you won't end up snitching on him. You should have known better than to trust these people."

At first, Carter was having a hard time trying to breathe but now he's laughing at me.

"Goodbye, you fool," he says the second I perceive someone behind me.

I whip around and see one of Xavier's suited gunmen aiming a gun at me, pulling the hammer back. But when the gunshot sounds I don't see any flashes of fire from the barrel.

I do, however, see the suit collapse to the ground and Jack standing behind him, a smoking gun in hand. He looks at me. "Something told me to follow you."

I walk over to him and place my hand on his shoulder as a display of my appreciation for the man. "You serve a very special purpose, Jack," I tell him.

In the zone of the loading and unloading of passengers my partners and I help load up Carter and the three remaining suited gunmen into the back of a police transport unit. "Y'all play nice now," I quip before closing the door.

The transport pulls off and I turn with my partners to head back to our cars. But among the gathered onlookers the press arrives, and so do Captain Brooks and our grizzly looking assistant chief of detectives, Patrick Mills. At our distance, we notice Ryan walking up to Mills—who was already shouting at him while pointing at Brooks.

"And here I am in a good mood after beating the crap out Xavier's henchmen," Toni says.

"We poked the bear," Rebecca says.

I take off my vest then throwing it into the back seat of the unmarked car I shared with Toni. Just as I did that, however, a taxi cab pulls up curbside and Faith hops out. The driver hops out as well, assisting her with the two duffle bags that were on the back seat with her. To say I was surprised would have been an understatement.

"Hey sweetheart," Faith says aloud as she approached us. "I'm glad I caught you."

"How did you know I was here?" I asked.

"A little birdie told me," Faith replies, smiling. "Now let's get out of here."

"Arrest that man!" Chief Mills' voice boomed over the air as he stampeded in our direction. Brooks and Ryan were doing their best to keep up with the fuming, white-haired man. It might be just my opinion, but it even appeared that Mills was turning bright red the more he talked—or rather shouted. "As a matter of fact arrest all them for obstructing an investigation!"

"What investigation sir?" Brooks inquired, stepping up beside the assistant chief.

"The Rosenfelts' murder investigation," Mills replied.

"But Chief, that's a closed case right now," Ryan explained. "The sheriff's office is over that. These detectives are unassigned and were just helping my unit with an apprehension per my request."

I'm glad the news cameras are here; the look on Mills' face is priceless. I imagine he came on the scene to chew everyone out and to enforce the department's decision concerning our squad's disbandment. But the ego trip he was on was totally unfounded and turned into egg on his face as local news reporters began shoving microphones in his direction. In addition, I knew that with Chief Mills present, there was also someone else present as well via news camera. My face was probably plastered all across his television screen at home, irking his nerves, and I was extremely comfortable with that. I took pleasure knowing that Frederick Xavier received word that I was still alive; much to his dismay.

"Brooks! What do you have to say about this?" Mills looked sternly in Captain Brooks' direction.

"Nothing, sir," Brooks answered, reaching out to shake my hand, then turning to walk away. "I'm retiring."

The chief's jaw dropped, and he appeared speechless. Ryan walks off as well then with my partners following behind him, looking back to bid Faith and I farewell.

The news reporters gather around closer, peppering the chief with questions he was unable to answer. I step closer toward Mills, leaning to whisper in his ear, "I quit."

Faith wraps her arm around my waist and we stroll off together into the airport.

"I told you I'd find you wherever you were, Sam," Faith tells me, nuzzling my neck.

"Yes, yes you did, sweetheart."

LAFAYETTE

The sky is a mild blue hue with stray, wispy clouds this saturday evening as I sit in a chaise lounge at pool side, being the only person watching my wife Faith swimming back and forth in the pool. Now I've known her for a long time but the way her beautiful physique cuts through the still waters now is absolutely mesmerizing. Every move, every turn she made was purposed and created artistic ripples and waves in the water.

Faith of course knows this because it is the reason she decided to take a swim in the first place. She does things like that for my benfit to give me something other than work to focus on. I appreciate it of course. Especially after the week I have had. I thought my faith had been tested in the past, but this past week made me look at everything with a new perspective. I knew that my return would bring about a change in the spiritual atmosphere. I also knew that my return would be both welcomed and hated. The city has a history of raising the corrupt, so when people like me are around trying to do some good, it sets the city on fire, it charges up evildoers to react aggressively.

It was my hope however, that I did not have to respond in kind. I consider my faith a very integral part of my being and as a result I try to use every method other than violence to get my point across, to start movements to better the community. Yet I know I have to go back after this vacation, I know I have to go back and continue the good fight—because it is expected of me. It's my job to make a difference.

My cell phone vibrates setting on the table beside my chair and I pick it up to answer the call. "Lafayette."

"Hey, Samuel," says an unmistakably, deep voice.

"Duke." I smile. "What news does the great cajun knight of justice share?"

"Well, you probably will believe it but, after you left, the judge called our offices and ordered us to arrest Fletcher and a couple of his senior deputies," Duke begins. "Also my bosses are suspended pending a full investigation. A special state prosecutor is being sent to oversee the offices here."

"I'm not surprised."

"Finally, something went right for a change."

I chuckle. "God won't always suffer evil, brother."

I can hear Duke shuffling papers around on his desk as he speaks. "All of this puts a wrench in Xavier's plans. Our acting mayor somehow has heard as well and will be holding a press conference on monday."

"Has anyone seen Xavier around?"

"I don't think so, Samuel. Last I think anyone saw him was that day you all saw him in his bar. But about that, be careful. You know he's after us."

"You be careful too, Duke. You still keep your pistol in the car?"

"You know it. Can't be too careful."

I hung on Duke's last statement deliberately noticing Faith climb out of the pool. She switched her hips while walking over to where I sat and picked up the large towel from the back of my chair.

"I think I'll visit the little ladies' room," Faith whispers in my ear, planting a kiss on my cheek, and then walking off.

"Samuel, you still there?" Duke says.

I reply hesitantly, "Umm…yes."

"How long will you be gone?"

"I don't know, I kind of quit my job when I left."

"I heard. But don't worry little brother. I'll take care of that. Apparently I have a little more clout now.

"Okay, brother."

Duke chuckles as he signs off. "See you when you get back."

"Peace." I close the phone off and set it aside, anxiously awaiting Faith's return. I briefly consider the Hawaiian print swimming trunks she made me wear and I feel slightly naked and embarrassed, feigning for one of my fitted, designer suits.

A moment later my cell rings again and I answer it just as Faith comes back and dives into the pool. "Lafayette,"

"That was quite the act you and your partners pulled off. I thought I actually had you a couple of times there," the familiar dark and foreboding voice says.

I sit forward abruptly, recognizing the voice. "How did you get this number?" I ask warily.

"Come now, Lafayette, give me more credit than that. Besides, you know I keep tabs on you," Xavier replies. "I do hope you're enjoying your well-deserved vacation."

"I appreciate your well wishes, not that your concern means anything to me." I glance around, looking for anything out of the ordinary.

"You and your family has caused me so much trouble—"

"Then you should quit, sir," I quip. "Your line of work is no good for your health, especially with you turning sixty-eight."

"The same could be said for you. You're smarter than most of your friends and family. So you can definitely see the advantages of not coming back again, am I right?"

"And let you take over the city? I think not, thank you very much," I say. "Oh and you should have sent better henchmen if you really wanted to do some damage."

"Maybe I come personally next time and we can dance under the pale moonlight."

"I do not fear you, Xavier," I say strongly.

"You should, Lafayette. Your wife does."

I glance at Faith, obliviously backstroking in the pool. "You leave her out of this."

"You know what I'm capable of, Lafayette. Get with your brother and take the deal that your father wouldn't—leave and never come back."

"No, and if any harm comes to her or the rest of my family I will find you and send you to hell myself."

Xavier laughs, "You're in no position to threaten me. I could reach out and kill you any time I wish."

"I answer to someone much bigger than you, Xavier. You can't touch me"

"Oh please, you think God is going to protect you? You think God will part the heavens and deflect a bullet from slicing open your skull? You are sorely mistaken. When it comes down to it, it will just be me and you, Lafayette."

I smile. "You have no idea what I'll bring to that fight, Xavier."

"I'm waiting."

To Be Continued....

We come to moments of accomplishments in our lives where we feel both humbled and relieved. Yet in those same moments, it is our family and friends that celebrate our accomplishments with us. I, myself know that there is no way I could have reached this milestone in my life without the support of my loved ones. So I dedicate this book, my first published work, to them—my family and my friends, those who have transcended to the next life as well as those who are yet present with me. I love you all.

--from the author's desk

CPSIA information can be obtained
at www.ICGtesting.com
Printed in the USA
LVOW10s0241140917
548700LV00021B/850/P